P9-BYT-469

THERE'S MORE TO MERLIN THAN MEETS THE EYE. . . .

The knights jumped back, drew their swords with a single ringing clang. . . .

Merlin stood apart and held up his hands as if praying. In a clear, forceful voice he said,

"Death to life,
Life to slaughter,
Arise, arise beasts of the forests,
Arise beasts of the fields,
Arise beasts of the air,
Forget your natures and become the wolf,
To kill a wolf."

And then, the wild boar, the tusked pig with its ribs stripped bare and its insides long since eaten, kicked its legs. . . .

The boar rolled over, stood on tiny hooves, and ran down the table toward Loki.

And not alone. All the dead creatures, pigs, birds, sheep, and goats all sprang back to hideous life, crisp skin crackling, blackened bones rasping, empty eye sockets gaping, up they came, up from the platters, clattered over their own discarded bones and rushed at the Norse god. . . .

We had frozen. The running had stopped. How could I run? How could I move? An old man had just brought dead animals to life. . . .

Look for other EVERWORLD titles

by K.A. Applegate:

EVER WORLD

ENTER THE ENCHANTED

K. A. APPLEGATE

SCHOLASTIC INC.
New York Toronto London Auckland Sydney
Mexico City New Delhi Hong Kong

If you purchased this book without a cover, you should be aware that this book is stolen property. It was reported as "unsold and destroyed" to the publisher, and neither the author nor the publisher received any payment for this "stripped book."

No part of this publication may be reproduced in whole or in part, or stored in a retrieval system, or transmitted in any form or by any means, electronic, mechanical, photocopying, recording, or otherwise, without written permission of the publisher. For information regarding permission, write to Scholastic Inc., Attention: Permissions Department, 555 Broadway, New York, NY 10012.

ISBN 0-590-87754-2

Copyright © 1999 by Katherine Applegate.
All rights reserved. Published by Scholastic Inc.
SCHOLASTIC and associated logos are trademarks and/or registered trademarks of Scholastic Inc.
EVERWORLD and associated logos are trademarks and/or registered trademarks of Katherine Applegate.

12 11 10 9 8 7 6 5 4 3 2 1   9/9 0 1 2 3 4/0

Printed in the U.S.A.

First Scholastic printing, September 1999

FOR MICHAEL
AND JAKE

CHAPTER
I

I was far from home.

As far from home as it is possible for a human being to get. Not a far place, a place apart, a place not touching reality, isolated.

Forget the normal. Normal was gone. Normal belonged to the real world.

There was magic here. Not magic like, "Ah, the moonlight was magic." Magic as in cause and effect didn't always cause or effect. The magic that negates all human knowledge, that invalidates ten thousand years of human learning.

Usually gravity worked, sometimes not. No way for that to be, of course; gravity isn't something you can turn on or off, if it were it wouldn't be gravity. If gravity could come and go, wax and wane, then things could fly when they could not possibly fly.

Like a dragon, maybe.

Can't possibly lift something as heavy and dense as a dragon, all that scaly skin, all that muscle, all that dense bone, not with wings, not with leathery wings like a pterodactyl. Wings that were not a tenth of what they had to be, not a hundredth of what was needed to raise this creature, this logic-killing monster into the air.

An elephant with wings. Dumbo, but not cute.

And fire. Could fire burn inside a living creature? Absurd. Ridiculous. Fire inside what, the belly? The intestines? The liver? Liquid flame spilling out of flesh, out of the monster's mouth, and that was supposed to be real? That was happening?

Fire needed air to burn; where was the air in the belly of the dragon? How could I understand anything when a creature as heavy as an elephant with liquid fire dribbling through its carnivore teeth was flying through the air?

I stood, rooted, yes rooted, like my toes had grown down into the dirt looking for water and now I couldn't move them because my feet were attached to the earth itself, or whatever passed for earth in this hideous, terrible place.

Run? How could I run from the dragon who pressed the tall trees down with the wind from its impossible wings and flamed the dry bushes in the night?

I could only stare. A miracle, that's what it was. A dragon.

"Damn it, April, run!" Jalil yelled.

His face was wild, not like Jalil, eyes wide, mouth stretched into some indecipherable shape, half grin, half howl.

Only Jalil cared. About me. And not all that much. David and Christopher were mesmerized, bewitched. More magic. Senna had gone to them, touched them, spoken to them, and they had lost themselves.

They stood with pitiful swords drawn, defiant and foolish, waving their impotent weapons up at the killer from the sky.

Jalil grabbed me, pulled me, dragged me. My feet moved, missed a step, tripped, up again, and now I ran. But not far. I had to stop, to see.

"Go back to your master, Merlin! Tell him I am not his!" Senna screamed. Her voice was a tinny, faraway shout, a sound all but erased by the vastness of the noise, the howling wind, the bellows sigh of leather wings, the crackle of underbrush bursting into flame.

The dragon inscribed slow, tight circles above the clearing, a living tornado, flying like a bird of prey, an eagle with green-and-yellow skin, with talons that could carry away a child, a man, a horse; what couldn't it carry with gravity meaningless?

Jalil and I huddled in the woods, unprotected by bowed trees and whipped grass and dirt flying in little cyclones. But the dragon didn't care for us. It watched Senna.

Have her! Take her! I cried silently. *This is her nightmare. Not mine. Not mine, you monster.*

I pressed my hands over my ears. I saw Jalil's mouth moving but did not hear his words.

Lower the dragon circled, lower, talons wide, ready to tear or take.

My hands slipped away from my ears. Reached for Jalil. Something solid to hold on to. Jalil, the prophet of reason.

David thrust upward with his sword, just missing the dragon's belly. Now Christopher, thrusting, stabbing, missing, a pathetic ballet. They were five-year-olds playing with sticks.

"Move aside, mortals," the dragon said, a bass rumble that vibrated the ground. "I was not summoned for you. Only for the witch."

Jalil's face, outlined, shadowed by the light of the dragon's fire. He shook his head, disbelieving.

Did it occur to you, at long last, Jalil, that all reason, all logic has been superseded?

"It spoke!" Jalil cried.

David and Christopher, two marionettes jerked up and down on their strings, stabbing, missing, falling, leaping up as though this were all a game, competing to see who could serve Senna's will.

Suddenly, the dragon dropped straight down. Senna leaped aside, plowed into Christopher, the two of them hit the dirt.

The dragon's wing, almost gentle, smothered David, pushing him down into the grass. The dragon's head snapped, reaching for Senna, missed.

Christopher was scrambling up from beneath her. The dragon snapped again, Senna twisted, bringing Christopher around as a shield.

It was almost quiet now. Weird after the dragon's wind. Almost silent but for David's shouts of "Senna! Senna!"

From somewhere a sound like the beating of hooves.

The dragon had a stubby horn on the end of its muzzle. It thrust the horn between Christopher and Senna and pried a yelling, fighting Christopher away from her.

Senna lay there, winded, helpless.

A terrified whinny. A horse?

"Hold!" a voice cried.

Near! I turned. Jalil with me. Four men on tall

horses. Four men in glistening armor, head to toe, hand to neck. Huge swords sheathed, lances laid across the armored necks of masked horses.

"Do not interfere, my lords," the dragon rumbled. "It is Merlin himself who has called me here."

One of the knights lifted the helmet from his head. Long black hair spilled down to his shoulders. Eyes that had to be blue looked over the scene, taking it all in.

"I honor Merlin as a great wizard," the knight said. "But you are a great liar, dragon. Even if you speak the truth, Merlin is not my master. You and I have our own matters of honor to address."

The dragon hesitated. Senna was helpless before him. David incapacitated. Christopher he tossed casually aside to land against an elm tree, a crumpled action figure, joints all twisted.

"This is not the time or the place," the dragon said. "I am in the service of Merlin the Magnificent."

The knight spurred his horse forward a few feet and seemed to notice me for the first time. He seemed puzzled by Jalil and me.

He walked his horse forward till he was just beside me. "I did not see you, my lady. Please forgive my failure to pay proper respects. I hope to atone for the oversight as soon as I have killed this evil dragon."

The dragon roared, but it was a sound of frustration more than a threat. "Another time, Galahad," the dragon said.

It flapped his wings, rose from the ground on its own private tornado, then swooped treacherously and suddenly toward the four knights.

Galahad (Galahad? *The* Galahad?) ducked and the dragon swept by overhead. It was the snake tail that caught me on the back of my head and knocked me staggering into Galahad's horse.

A mailed fist reached down, grabbed a hasty handful of my shirt as the dragon flew off into the night.

The world was spinning, swirling, darkening at the edges. My knees buckled but the knight held me up effortlessly.

I saw straight black hair. Steel-gray eyes, not blue. A face . . . a face . . .

"Hi," I said. "I'm April."

Then the world went black. But not a fade-out. Only a quick cut to a very different scene.

"April?"

I blinked. Class. Drama class. Eyes all watching me, some bored, most expectant.

"April?" the teacher said. "Do you need the line?"

"The line?" I echoed weakly. "No. No." I shook off the sudden transition. Unconscious in Everworld, back in the real world. Back in my real life, picking it up from, well, from myself.

Class. A dramatic reading. Me and Jerry Bell. I was Ophelia.

It was not my first sudden, shocking return to a life that played on without me in this other reality.

Not my first transition. Just the first one I came close to regretting.

CHAPTER
II

My world had recently gone deeply weird. One minute life was life. Friends, family, school, church, the play I was rehearsing. The next minute it had become fear and violence, an anarchic lawlessness that extended down to the level of the fundamental physical laws.

I've known magic in my life. The magic that comes as an unexpected bonus from real, true things. The applause of an audience is magic. A kiss can be magic. Or not. It was magic when I saw my cousin's little baby girl for the first time.

That's the magic of the real world. That's my magic.

But I had grown up with Senna. We share a father. He had shared two women: my mother, and Senna's. Senna came into our family at an early age; I was four and, as far as I ever could see, she was treated as an equal by my mom. Despite the fact that she was the child of my dad's affair.

They lied to me about it, of course. Told me that Senna had always been my sister, that she had simply arrived in a different way. Twisting my reality, trying to make me believe that what I knew was wrong. Anything rather than explain the truth.

Later I understood. People being weak, people doing wrong, that's part of life. And I tried to accept this new person, this strange little girl almost my age.

But Senna didn't want acceptance. She wanted nothing from me. She was complete and apart. And for her, somehow, though I never came to grips with it, never faced it, the world was different.

From that time on I'd suspected that even in our world, even in the real world, there were degrees of reality. Not the total "throw Newton and Galileo out the window" magic of Everworld, but the tiny gaps in the structure of reality. Just peeks and glimpses of strangeness, all somehow caused by or coming from Senna.

In our shared rooms, in our shared home growing up, Senna was different from me. Different from everyone I knew. We had become two factions, two political parties, two opposing world-

views, Senna and I. She was the party of Weird.
Me? I wanted to be an actress. A different weird-
ness, maybe, but one that came from a need to
represent the truth.

Or maybe that's just what I told myself. Maybe,
like so many wanna-be actors and already-am actors, I just wanted to escape a life I saw as boring.

Boring in contrast to the compelling, exotic
creature who lived in the room on the far side of
our adjoining bathroom.

As she grew and I grew we did not grow together, my half sister and me. And yet, on that
damp, gray morning down by the lake, I was
there, drawn, transported, pulled, compelled,
maybe just curious, but I was there. Me and David
and Jalil and Christopher.

Summoned. Called. That's how it felt. How else
to explain that we were all there, all where we'd
never have been otherwise, but for her?

We could have just watched when Fenrir,
Loki's monstrous wolf son, broke the barrier be-
tween Everworld and the real world and dragged
Senna away. We should have just watched. But
we ran. Ran in the wrong direction, it now seems.
We ran to her.

It felt at the time like we were rescuing her,
David in the lead, of course, yelling "Senna!"
with his mind churning up the visions of hero-

ism that make up so much of his difficult person-
ality.

We ran, toward a wolf the size of a bus, toward
Senna, toward a universe that could not possibly
exist, but for the fact that it did.

We don't exactly know what Everworld is. We
know it is a universe constructed by the fugitive
gods of ancient Earth. We know that recently
alien immortals have found their way in. Inter-
lopers in a private chat room. We know that one
of these alien gods is Ka Anor, god of the Hetwan.
We know Ka Anor scares the heck out of the es-
tablished gods. Scares them like nothing ever has
before.

And we know that the four of us are there in
this lunatic asylum: me, David, Jalil, and Christopher. We know Senna is the reason we're here.
But that doesn't explain anything, either.

None of us knows. None of us understands.

David doesn't do "theories," of course. That
wouldn't really work for him. He wants us all to
see him as some kind of direct, straightforward
man-of-action type. That's his self-image. What
he wills himself to be. But he wears his bruises
and scars on the outside, out in plain view where
anyone, at least any girl or woman, can see them.

David thinks no one sees the insecurity, no one

sees the uncertainty. If he just keeps talking tough and gritting his teeth and racing toward each new danger, we'll all forget the failings we've seen; we'll buy the image. We'll forget how he broke down before Loki. We'll somehow not see the shadows cast by earlier failings, failings that gnaw at his insides during every quiet moment. We'll never ask whether his own fear is what makes him brave.

It's what makes him comical and fascinating and even a little wonderful, all at the same time.

Christopher? Christopher keeps trying to convince himself that life is one big sitcom. Like he'd be able to make sense of it all if he could just go back and watch the entire *I Love Lucy* oeuvre.

The world is too complicated for Christopher. Not that he's not intelligent, he is. But he needs the world to make sense, and he needs it to fit, to be predictable. He wants the big pendulum to swing in a narrow arc, not too far. And when it doesn't, he takes the world and forces it into place, organizes it with humor and narrow-mindedness. He'll chop off the ends of the arc.

Too sad? Kill it with a joke. Is someone too near to touching his heart? Push the person away with a harsh cheap shot guaranteed to alienate.

Now, Jalil does do "theory." Jalil does little else.

And of the four of us, he remains the most opaque to me. Also the most interesting.

Jalil believes in nothing but a reality that can be demonstrated in a laboratory, written up in a paper, and then replicated in another lab. So he says, and I believe him. I have the respect for him that believers sometimes have for nonbelievers. He's not lukewarm, not half in and half out, not just covering his ass, not pretending to a belief system he doesn't live.

Jalil looks out for himself, so he says, and that I don't entirely believe. It's him I look to instinctively for support.

All of us are involved in some way with Senna. David as her most recent conquest. Christopher as the spurned lover. Me as her half sister. And Jalil? No one knows. No one but Jalil, and Senna.

David loves Everworld, Christopher wants out, and Jalil talks about parallel universes, and hey, that's as good an explanation as any, I guess. Not that it really explains very much.

When Jalil talks about parallel universes I picture two soap bubbles floating through the air. One contains all we know to be real. The other contains an entirely separate set of laws and truths and realities.

Fall asleep over there, in Everworld, lose consciousness, and suddenly we're back in the real world. That seems to be the key. Consciousness there keeps us there.

But knowing that, or at least believing that, doesn't tell me how I can avoid going back, how I can grab on and hold on to my own world.

And I do want to hold on.

CHAPTER
III

I finished reading the scene for the class. Not my best performance, I was a little distracted. A little distracted by the fact that I, or some version of me, my twin, had just been saved from a dragon by Galahad. Sir Galahad, I suppose I should say. Sir Laurence Olivier, Sir Anthony Hopkins, Sir Galahad.

Yeah.

And now I was here. Class, with the clock on the wall above the door, the good old time-only-moves-one-direction clock ticking away the minutes. I had been here all along, of course. Had been here and there.

It was one of the paradoxes of this lunatic life. You knew when the two "yous" first rejoined in the real world because you'd get this sudden news flash, this CNN Breaking News: The other you is about to become a human sacrifice, or dragon food, or prey to some alien.

The bell rang.

This just in: April O'Brien is losing her mind.

"You did great, really brought the character to life," my friend Magdalena said as we filed out into the hall.

I sighed. "Magda, you're sweet, but if you're ever going to make a career out of acting you'll have to learn how to lie."

This was my life. This was me. Don't let it affect you, April. Don't let it take over your life. This is you, the real you. Who cares what that other April is doing or having done to her?

That's her. Not you.

"Acting? Hey, I want to direct. But, just between us, honey, you do seem a little spacey. I know what it is, too. It's the vegetarian thing. See, I'm sorry, I know it's not my business, but sometimes I think you need to eat a little meat." She batted her eyes suggestively. "Mario comes to mind. 'Cause that's all beef, baby."

I laughed. The laughter seemed fake. Her face, fake. The room, the hallway, the kids all crowding around, sauntering or rushing to their next class, fake.

I was in the middle of two lives at once. I had all my memories of being here, and all my mem-

ories of being there. I remembered Mario asking
me out last night. And I remembered Galahad
grabbing my shirt just moments ago. Both real.
Both interesting.

Mario was another drama guy. And he was actually straight. And Magda was right, he was all
dark, brooding eyes and smooth chest and full
lips. Antonio Banderas as a senior.

"He has bad teeth," I said. We reached my
locker and I stepped out of the river of moving
bodies and grabbed the steel shore.

"He can have that fixed. Everyone in Holly-
wood has their teeth fixed. Brad Pitt had awful
teeth. Brad Pitt had medieval teeth."

The locker combination. Did I still know it?
How could I? How could I remember something
so trivial when my head was filled with the
dragon's liquid fire?

"Now how on Earth do you know anything
about Brad Pitt's teeth?" I asked. Going through
the motions. Saying the right things. Like a long-
running play where I'd done the same lines a
thousand times.

Magda ignored that question since she found it
inconvenient. "You don't want Mario, I'll take
him. I'm not proud, I'll take your castoffs. I'll take
him, and by the time I'm done with him you
won't want him back."

I spun the numbers on my locker. Twelve. Six. Twenty-seven. Still there in my brain.

"What do you know about Sir Galahad?"

She looked blank. "Is that some guy's nickname?"

"No, I mean the real Galahad."

"There's no real Galahad," Magda said. "Just a story. King Arthur and Camelot and all. Although Galahad has a separate story: You know, the whole quest for the Holy Grail. He was supposed to be the perfect knight."

Magda tries hard to pass herself off as a sort of tough-girl slut. In reality, or at least in a part of her reality, she's a National Merit Scholar who uses her intellect mainly for sleazy double entendres. But then you ask her something obscure and she has more information than you'd expect from a girl who wears midriff-baring everything to show off the strand of barbed wire tattooed around her waist.

"Galahad? He's a myth."

"Yeah," I said.

"But if the point is you're looking for a man of steel with a big lance . . ."

I pulled out my new chemistry book. My old one had gone across with me. We'd traded it to the Coo-Hatch, an alien race of obsessive metallurgists.

"How about dragons?"

Magda closed my locker door and gave me her serious look. "April, what's up with you?"

I spun the lock. Held on to the little numbered dial. Stared at the blank steel door. I could tell her. I could. I could say, "Magda, I am split in two, spending one life here and most of a life in an alternate universe."

And she'd nod and pretend to believe me and slowly but inexorably pull away, put distance between us, be unavailable, busy, "Sorry but I already promised to hang with Tyra, no, I don't think I'm in the mood to go shopping . . ."

And word would spread: April? Nuts.

Insanity is the limit of friendship.

I tell my friends everything. Every dream, every disappointment, every crush, every fantasy. I tell them things that go right to the heart of who I am, things that I could not stand to have known by strangers. Everything, except about Senna, except about our childhood together, but everything else, everything from my real life. Magda, Elspeth, Jennifer, Tyra, Alison, Becka, 'Suela, they knew me, I knew them, to various degrees.

My friends were mostly drama club. We performed together. We took classes together. All those lame "pretend you're a tree" exercises, we did all that together. When we had to act scared, or act happy, or act hurt or despairing; when we had to imagine ourselves as mothers or old women or prostitutes or businesswomen or Danish princesses driven mad by loss; when we had to reach deep to come up with raw emotions, we could do that because we were we. Because we trusted one another and supported one another.

What was I without friends? Something, I was sure. I mean, I wouldn't disappear if I was alone. But I'd never tried it.

"April, whatever it is, you can tell me, it's me, it's Magda, come on, spill it, you'll feel better."

I forced a smile. Not just any smile, either, a smile was never just a smile. I gave Magda a Julia-Roberts-lying-through-her-teeth-in-*My-Best-Friend's-Wedding* smile.

"Just wondering how happy I should make Mario Saturday night."

Chapter IV

School.

Rehearsal. We were doing *Rent*. We were doing it in a week, and I was playing Mimi. She's a junkie with HIV. Not exactly a case of playing myself. And the singing . . . I had to find a wildness, a reckless despair that had never been part of me.

And then, I had a date. Mario. He was going to pick me up at 8:00. We were going to see *La Dolce Vita* down in the city at a theater that showed old films.

Then we'd get some coffee, maybe a snack somewhere, and talk. We'd talk about the movie, and about *Rent*, and about acting, and I'd tell him about going to New York and seeing Kevin Spacey in *The Iceman Cometh*, and Mario would tell me about meeting John Malkovich once when he came to Chicago to direct a play.

Then we'd drive home up Lake Shore Drive and he'd act cool, and I'd act ditzy even though I was trying to be cool, and then the big moment would come, the big kiss, and would there be tongue or no tongue?

"Why bother to go if you already know every scene?" I berated myself. "You don't know: It might not happen that way."

I stared at my closet. It contained three types of clothing: stuff that made me look fat, stuff that made me look desperate, and stuff my dad would actually approve of.

Wardrobe. Then makeup. Then on to the set to deliver my practiced lines. "He was amazing! He was born to play that role!" Or, "I've always felt that people underrate Susan Sarandon." Or, "No, I, um, well, Nicole Kidman in *Eyes Wide Shut*? Um, I uh, I guess I could play a part like that."

Blush.

"Stop it, April," I snapped at the reflection of my half made-up face. "Just stop it. He's a nice guy. He has talent. He's hot. So shut up and enjoy the date."

The clock showed 7:49. Eleven minutes, if he was on time. Eleven long minutes. More, if he was late.

I applied lip gloss.

Any minute now. Any minute now, Mario. Any minute now I would open my eyes over there, open my eyes and discover . . . what?

I couldn't let this happen. I couldn't let my real life be eaten up by the knowledge that I had another life entirely.

I was getting angry now. Where was he? It was 8:00. No, it was 8:01. He was late. At any moment I, a part of me, would suddenly be there, not here. Only I would be here, too. Half of me would go on a date. Maybe the other me was already there, already gone? How would I know until she, me, I, reappeared with yet another update?

"Oh, hi, April, have a nice date with Mario? Yeah? Well, guess what Galahad and I did?"

Madness!

I sat down on the little chair outside my walk-in closet. Sat there in my not-too-easy outfit and stared down at my bare toes cold on the wood floor.

Here. There. It was too much. One life was enough. I didn't need two.

"Go away and leave me alone," I whispered. The clock said 8:07.

I felt alone. Had she left? I couldn't know.

A discreet knock on my door. "April? Your date is here."

My mom. She still had her "mourning" voice. We were mourning the disappearance of Senna. Weeks had passed in the real world. The agreed story, the myth we all paid lip service to was that Senna had always been independent, that she had gone off on her own, no doubt in search of her birth mother.

We were all very worried. My mom. My dad. Long faces, soft voices, downcast eyes, shuffling tread. Very worried. My dad would turn on *Frasier* and feel like he had to say, "We could use some cheering up."

Lately, the last couple of days we'd begun the segue into the "I'm sure she's fine, she always did take care of herself" phase.

The police had no body, after all. No dead Senna had turned up in a ditch. And frankly, everyone was ready to move on, tired of the tedious job of playing sad and distressed.

I dreamed of sitting down at the dinner table and saying, "Let's all cut the b.s., Mom, Dad, we're all relieved she's gone. Besides, I know exactly where Senna is."

But that wasn't in the script.

What was in the script was my mom saying, "Honey, I think it's good you're starting to have fun again. Senna would want us to move on with our lives."

I squeezed her hand. She squeezed back. We gave each other smiles tinged with loss.

I went out with Mario. We saw the movie. We talked. I had a mocha and a pannini made with hummus. We talked some more. We drove home. Mario stuck his tongue in my mouth and his hand inside my blouse. I stopped him. I don't even know why. Half my life I was in hell, and the other half I was still trying to be a good girl.

I tried to remember every detail because Magda and Elspeth, Jennifer and Alison, Becka and Tyra and 'Suela would want the details, down to the last word and sensation and private thought.

I got home a little after midnight and moments later, just as I was climbing into a steaming-hot shower, I was there.

CHAPTER V

Bed.

Four thick, dark oak bedposts, a sort of feather comforter over me, no sheets, just a soft, down-filled comforter under me and the same over me and over that a coverlet or something, mostly maroon with faded traces of gold.

There was a fire in a huge stone hearth, more coals than flames.

The smell of salt water. The sea. We were near the sea. Were those waves I heard? Waves crashing on rocks? Or just an echo, a distortion?

The walls were stone, granite, I suppose, I'm not a geologist. The floor was stone softened by a scattering of reeds and, hey, flower petals. Well, that was nice.

There was a faded tapestry on the wall. I think it showed a guy in armor kneeling before a woman in white. No way to tell for sure with the colors all washed out.

There was a single window, tall and narrow, a pointed arch at the top, like something you'd see in a Gothic cathedral.

It was day. Bright blue filled the window. Morning light. That's what it felt like. But the light had little impact on the gloom inside. It barely grayed the blackness in the high corners of the room, twenty feet above me.

I wasn't wearing sneakers.

I threw back the covers, a sudden, convulsive gesture. I sighed. I still had my clothes on. A weird little outfit consisting of the clothes I'd been wearing down at the lake and the odds and ends I'd picked up from Vikings and Aztecs.

I was a bag lady. All I needed was a shopping cart full of cans and a personal relationship with the Martian high council.

I tried to slow my racing, panicked heart. (Would I ever get used to these transitions? Would I have to?) Things couldn't be too bad: I was in a feather bed and had my clothes on.

I swung out of bed and almost fell, surprised by the distance to the floor. There were my sneakers. I stuck my feet in and tied them quickly.

The headache exploded about then. Pounding, pounding, but fading as I closed my eyes and rubbed my temples. It was the remains of a much worse headache.

I felt the back of my head where the dragon's tail had slapped me. There was a bump the size of the yolk of a sunny-side up egg.

"Okay, you have clothes, you have shoes, and there's your backpack. This is good, April. This is better than some Everworld wake-ups."

I was alone, I was pretty sure of that. Where were David and Christopher and Jalil?

I grabbed my pack, fished for the bottle of Advil, and swallowed two dry.

I headed for the door. It was chilly in the room, despite the fire.

It took me a few seconds to figure out the door handle. There was no knob. Just a sort of iron latch. I lifted it and, wincing at the creaking sound, pulled the door toward me.

A hallway. Stone walls, stone floor, narrow, high.

"Hello?"

No answer. Part of me wondered if there was a phone by the bed. I could call down to the front desk. "Hi, I don't know my room number, but could you send up a pot of coffee and some toast? And some ice water?"

Old Marx Brothers movie, maybe 1929 or whatever. Groucho's at the desk of a hotel. Phone rings. Caller asks for some ice water. Groucho says, "Ice water? You want ice water? I'll send up some onions. That'll make your eyes water."

Bad pun. But it was 1929. Probably not Groucho at the front desk of this place. Maybe a troll. Maybe Loki. No, I'd be dead.

"Shut up, April, you're babbling because you're scared."

"Shut up? I wasn't even talking out loud."

"Well, you are now. You're talking to yourself."

I stepped cautiously out into the hallway. Left or right? I heard nothing to guide me. But the hallway ended in darkness to the right and was bisected by one of the tall, arched windows to my left.

"Go into the light, April," I muttered.

I padded silently down the hall, stepping unconsciously over the cracks between the stones. After all, I didn't want to break my mother's back.

A door, identical to mine. I leaned close.

"Hello?"

Was I up too early? Was that it? No, I must have been unconscious a long time. A concussion? Did things like that just go away or was some big blood clot just waiting to bust loose and kill me?

Dead of a stroke. Probably not the most likely

thing to worry about in Everworld. So many other, more dramatic ways to die.

I knocked on the door. Nothing. I turned away intending to look out of the window. Then I heard a creak. Spun around and saw David, wearing pants and no shoes and no shirt.

"Kind of early," he said. He rubbed his left eye with the heel of his hand and then had trouble opening that eye. "You okay?" he asked.

Don't look at his chest.

"David, where are we?"

"Galahad's castle. Or one of them. I think he has more."

"So are we . . . what are we? I mean, are we prisoners? Or are we guests?"

I said, don't look at his chest, it's tacky. It's the kind of thing a guy would do.

David raised his eyebrows. "Yes. All of the above, I think."

"Are the others okay?"

"Yeah. Well, Jalil is. Christopher got faced at the banquet last night. Tried to outdrink Sir Perceval. I think he's in his room puking. Christopher, I mean. How's your head? Galahad's doctor wanted to put leeches on your face and neck. I convinced him not to. Hope that wasn't too presumptuous or whatever."

I shuddered. "No, you have permission to stop anyone from putting leeches on me at any time. Jeez, so . . . so what do we do?"

David glanced back over his shoulder, then lowered his voice to a whisper. "We have to bust out of here. Merlin is coming."

I laughed, then regretted it for the needle of pain it sent through my head. "There's a phrase you don't hear very often: 'Merlin is coming.'"

David didn't laugh. His eyes clouded. He seemed uncertain. Distracted.

And then I saw the hand come sliding over his bare shoulder and down over his chest.

She leaned into view behind him, face almost resting on his shoulder.

Senna.

Chapter
VI

"Well, well," I said.

"It's good to see you," Senna said. She slid out from behind David.

I didn't know what to say. "Well, well" had pretty much used up my possibilities. We had followed Senna into Everworld and been following her, one way or another, ever since. Following without really knowing why, or even what or whom we were following.

We'd finally caught up with her, or she with us, and she'd had just enough time to sidestep Jalil's pointed questions, when the dragon attacked.

Then I thought of something to say. "David, maybe they can get you another room. One without snakes."

Senna laughed her mocking laugh. Then her

eyes went all sincere. I swear, I worry she's a better actress than I'll ever be.

"April, you're mad because you don't understand what's happening."

"You're right I don't understand," I admitted. "So why don't you explain?"

"I only know part of the picture," she said. "But what I know is so . . . so incredible, so powerful . . ."

I think I must have rolled my eyes. Not consciously. It's just my standard response to b.s.

"It's all right," David said reassuringly. "Don't worry, you just don't understand."

"Has she explained it all to you, David?"

Again the wrinkling of his brow, the confused look in his dark eyes.

"David knows that what I'm doing is important and that I need his support," Senna said earnestly. But then I saw the cocky smirk that hid beneath the surface. Not such a great actress, really.

"Where are Jalil and Christopher?" I asked. "Maybe they're still both men."

It was meant as an insult. It was meant to make David mad, wake him up. Senna seemed to have some power over David. Was it strong, unshakable?

David's eyes narrowed.

"Don't try to provoke him," Senna said.

"Don't try to provoke me," David said.

I wanted to throw up. Or throw something. He was her puppet. She might as well have her arm inserted up his butt.

"Think I'll go say hi to the other guys," I said. I turned away. Headed down the hall. Heard Senna move. Heard her call to me.

"Don't fight me, April. You think I'm bad, evil, but you're wrong. There are real evils here. I'm doing all I can to resist them. You don't have to like me but you should at least believe that. I saved your lives. Why would I do that if I wanted to hurt you?"

It was a good point. She'd spoken with sincerity and feeling. A nice little speech. It sounded rehearsed. I stopped walking.

"Why would you save us? Because you need us. You want to use us. That's why we're here. Because you need us for something."

She was wearing a silky sort of nightgown with wide sleeves, a deep neckline that hung loose from her narrow, vulnerable shoulders, and slits up the sides to show off her legs. Something that just happened to be in Sir Galahad's closet? Where did she find something like that?

I blinked and looked again. The neckline had risen. No. That wasn't possible. And the fabric was more opaque. I shook it off. Bizarre. My mind playing tricks.

She spread her hands wide. "I'm the victim here, April. I'm the one who was snatched up by Fenrir, carried away. I'm the one who simply appeared alongside that murderous filth Huitzilopoctli. I'm the one Merlin's mercenary dragon was trying to kill."

I walked back to her, mostly to show I wasn't scared of her. "How did you get away from Fenrir?"

"I . . . I didn't. I mean, it wasn't me. I just happened to —"

"You want me to believe you, Senna? Start telling the truth."

"The truth is dangerous to you. The less you know, the better. I am trying to keep you alive, all of you."

I blinked. Was that the truth? Was she right?

She moved closer, reached for my hand, inches from touching me.

Maybe she was right, maybe I was being a paranoid fool. She'd never actually done anything evil that I knew of. I was jumping to conclusions and —

"Don't let her touch you!" Christopher yelled.

I jerked my hand away.

"That's how she does it." He came up behind me. I glanced back. Jalil was with him.

"Still jealous, Christopher?" Senna mocked him. "Just because I chose David to keep me warm through the night and not you?"

"You bet I'm jealous. Totally jealous," Christopher admitted. "But that doesn't change what you are."

Senna pushed away from David. She stepped over to the tall window, gazed out in a parody of "thoughtful consideration," then turned her gaze on us.

She was the picture-perfect waif, the little lost girl, the "someone take care of me, I'm just ever-so-fragile" creature of fashion photo layouts. Lank blond hair, gray, sorrowful eyes, full lips. All she lacked to be the next Calvin Klein girl was the blankly stupid model look in her eyes. Give her credit: Senna's eyes were alive, focused, intense, glittering. Greedy.

"No hands," she said, holding up her hands. "No magic. Happy now?"

David didn't look happy. He looked sick. Lost. A puppy whose master has yelled "Stay!" and gone off alone.

"Okay, you're all upset that you're here. Okay, you're all mad at me. Okay, you all think I'm up to something. You're right, I am," she said.

"What?" Jalil asked reasonably.

"Changes are coming. Cataclysmic changes.

The old order will be thrown down, a new order will rise up in its place. The Hetwans' god, Ka Anor, is a revolution, a terror. I can affect how things happen. I can't stop it, but I can make it good instead of bad. I'm sorry if you don't like my methods, but I do what I have to do."

For a second I wavered.

Then Jalil, in his dry, doesn't-impress-me voice, said, "That's pretty good: an entire paragraph saying absolutely nothing."

"Everything I say you meet with hostility and suspicion," Senna said sadly. "Fine. Merlin will come soon. Galahad will give Merlin what he wants: Me. Then how do you suppose you'll ever get back home?"

"You can get us back home?" Christopher snapped.

"I and no one else," she said. "You want to go home, back to your lives? Permanently, I mean, not drifting back and forth like unhappy ghosts? I can make that happen. But not if Merlin gets me first."

That, at last, was a point I had to listen to. It had the ring of truth. Senna had carried us along with her to Everworld. Maybe she could get us home again.

"Let David go," I said.

Senna looked surprised. "Aww, you want him

for yourself, April?" She shrugged. "You have excellent taste. He's very gentle underneath it all."

"That's not it. Just let him go. We need to think about what you've said. He's one of us."

"I'm one of you."

"Let him go."

Full, pouty, Cover Girl lips drew back, an animal baring its teeth. Then she sighed, letting it go with an unspoken promise to take care of me later. "Already done. He's all yours."

David rubbed his eyes like he'd had a flash go off in his face. When he pulled his hands away his eyes were wary. And a little embarrassed. He looked around like he was wondering where his shirt was.

Senna stabbed her finger at me. "Just remember this, April: I die, you never leave."

A nice exit line. But it was spoiled by the way she froze, cocked her head to the side, as if listening to voices in her head. Her pale face grew paler still. Real emotion, maybe the only real emotion she could feel, revealed itself on her face. Fear.

"No," she whispered. "He's here."

"Who?" Jalil asked.

At that moment the door at the far, gloomy end of the hallway opened wide. A file of men with helmets, tall pikes, and swords belted at their waists marched toward us.

Their officer swaggered importantly in front, but he was shaken, worried. And not by us. Something had gone wrong. Something very bad was happening.

He came to a stop a few feet from us, eyes on Senna, wary. He bowed without ever letting Senna out of his sight.

"My lord has commanded me to say that he would be honored by your attendance in the great hall."

"So, I guess Merlin is here, huh?" Christopher asked. "Cool."

"The wizard, yes," the captain of the guard said. "And the god."

CHAPTER
VII

I was given clothing for the big meal. A full-length dress or tunic. Low-cut square neckline, totally wrong for my bra straps, deep sleeves.

I actually worried that Senna would be better dressed. A stupid thing to worry about at that particular moment, with a harried, scared serving woman adjusting the shoulders and the neckline. But strange things will pop into your head at the wrong times. I considered it a good sign. A sign my brain was hanging onto normalcy in spite of everything.

The serving woman didn't like my slipping my backpack on, but she didn't argue too much. Mostly she muttered under her breath about gods coming to a banquet, and what would come of it, nothing good, she was sure.

We assembled a few minutes later, back in the hallway. The guys were wearing what they'd worn in: a motley collection of their own, normal clothes and Viking animal skins. Only Senna and I had been dressed up. And yes, she looked better than me.

It all gave me a queasy little feeling. What kind of castle was this Galahad running? He stocked women's clothing? What next, a circular bed, mirrors on the ceiling, and X-rated videos?

I had this flash of Galahad as Austin Powers. "Welcome to Everworld, baby, it's shagadelic."

But that wasn't my greatest concern. The captain of the guard had said we'd be dining with a god. So far the gods I'd met didn't make me want to meet more.

"Kind of early for lunch, and late for breakfast," Christopher muttered. "I mean, what is it, like, ten? Ten-thirty?"

"Brunch," I said.

"I imagine when a god shows up and says, 'I'm hungry,' you eat right then, whatever time it is," Jalil said. "Besides, they don't exactly have clocks."

David was quiet. It disturbed me. Was he still under Senna's control? Or was he himself again?

I shot a glance at Senna, at the side of her face.

Lips pressed thin, face tight. She was scared. Well, that was good at least. Maybe.

Unless she was telling the truth and we needed her to escape from Everworld.

We marched along behind the captain, flanked by his guards. The men-at-arms kept their distance from Senna, leaving gaps around her, but keeping her hemmed in just the same.

Heavy boots rang on flagstone. Our sneakers were silent. I was wearing sneakers and a full-length dress. Like some suburban housewife wrangling the kids into the supermarket who threw on the last clean thing she had.

We marched, and I do mean marched, because it's impossible to be surrounded by people marching and not fall into it yourself.

We passed a window that framed a stunningly beautiful view: gray-green waves foaming around jumbled rocks, the ocean, a blue sky. So beautiful my heart was torn between optimism (I mean, what could go wrong with the sun shining and the waves crashing?) and the gloomy feeling that this sight was the last sweet vision I'd ever see.

We marched into the great hall of the castle.

Lots of granite. No shortage of rock in this place. Walls, floors, arched ceiling, all stone. You could feel it weighing down on you, smothering the air. The walls had been painted a sort of ocher color and were hung with tapestries similar to the one in my room. None of it helped. This room would never be cozy.

There was a fireplace so big you would be happy to have a walk-in closet half the size. The fire blazed from what had to have been a tree trunk. The heat seemed to reach about half the distance to the massive table.

It was cold in the room. Not surprising, given that we were in the middle of a heap of stones with no glass in the windows.

Three dogs wandered back and forth, anxious, anticipating food. I had no desire to pet them.

Servants leaned against the wall on either side of the fireplace. There were three tables. A main one like the one in da Vinci's *Last Supper*, then two smaller ones at right angles from the main table.

All the tables were set with white cloths, water bowls, a silver ship thing that seemed to hold salt, knives, spoons, and goblets of varying degrees of magnificence. Some were gold-encrusted, with what looked like rubies and emeralds and probably *were* rubies and emeralds. I kept having to remind myself this was not some elaborate stage set. This was real. Or as real as Everworld could be. At the other end of the spectrum were rude bowls carved out of wood.

The chairs, too, were mismatched, varying from three massive, near-throne things at the main table, down to what looked like short bar stools built by carpenters who'd worked with butter knives for tools.

There was no attempt at equality. There was the A-list, the B-list, and the peasants. Or maybe Galahad, like any host, only had so many good chairs. The stools were the equivalent of the folding chairs you bring up from the basement when extra people show up.

"I'm guessing we sit there," Christopher said, pointing to a set of particularly K-mart dishes and chairs.

We were not alone in the room. A dozen people, all men — mostly bearded, hair down to their shoulders, or in some cases, cut short, all adorned with at least one jewel, a ring or a brooch or a sort of pendant — milled and talked in whispers and sidelong glances.

The sidelong glances were for Senna. Not welcoming looks, either. Expressions ranged from fearful to lascivious to thoughtful.

They were a sturdy, confident group. One in particular was quite handsome, pretty even. Others were older and rougher.

"Percy, dude!" Christopher called out.

One of the knights gave him a nod of the head,

but otherwise kept his distance. We were with the witch.

"That guy can hold his ale," Christopher reported. "See the good-looking guy? You know who that is? That's Sir Gawain. That's Sir Kay and Sir Gareth." He shook his head wonderingly. "So cool."

The names were supposed to mean something to me, but didn't. Christopher acted like he'd just pointed out the cast of *Buffy*. "Do we sit or what?" I asked.

Christopher shook his head. "We did this last night when we first got to the castle. Just a light snack then, plus adult beverages. You wait for the main boys to show up. Galahad comes last. His house. Then we sit. We drink. We eat. We throw stuff on the floor. We fart and belch and scratch ourselves in private places. We talk about wenches and laugh real loud. You'll love it. Kind of like the school cafeteria back in junior high."

Jalil made quiet introductions all over again, obviously as impressed as Christopher. "That's Sir Perceval, Sir Kay, Sir Gawain . . ."

My brain clicked. "What is, 'Knights of the Round Table, Alex?'" I asked *Jeopardy*-style.

"You got it," Jalil said. "The Knights of the freaking Round Table. King Arthur's boys."

"What are they doing in Everworld? They aren't immortals. They aren't gods."

"Hey, you need someone to rescue virgins and kill dragons, which covers both you girls," Christopher said, batting his eyes at me and Senna.

Jalil smothered a grin. "Why don't you ask them, April? My one hope is we'll get some answers now. We're having brunch with Merlin, Galahad, the Knights of the Round Table, and some god. We ought to at least get a clue."

"They're legends, though, not gods," Christopher said, echoing my point. "I mean, if legends are here, too, am I gonna get to meet Michael Jordan, or what?"

David remained quiet. Deep within himself. Senna stood away from us, staring into the fire, shielding herself from the hard looks all around us. Tense. She was waiting for something. Fearful of something.

Personally, I was torn between fear and the more basic feeling of hunger. I was starving. Starving and with nothing really specific to be afraid of. Yet.

A big door at the far end of the hall was thrown open. And in walked the old man with the once-blond hair and beard. He wore a robe, dark blue, but not the goofy curly-toed slippers you'd expect on some goofy book wizard. He wore boots crusted with mud and pants tucked in at the top, also muddy and only now beginning to dry. There was a sword at his side.

Merlin.

We'd met him before, briefly, at the temple of Huitzilopoctli. Other things had seemed more important at the time.

I should have asked Magda about him. Or looked him up in a book. Something. These people were all myths, legends. But they were real enough here and now. Real and with real weapons.

The knights nodded with exaggerated casualness, showing respect for the wizard but not fear. Or so they thought. The fear came in the way they parted for the old man, took a half step back without really thinking about it.

That's one of the things you learn to do when you study acting. You watch the nonverbal cues. That's what gives a performance depth. The knights were all like, "Hey, Merlin, what's up?" But get past the easy words and bluff tone and you saw faces drawn back, bodies turned at an angle to protect the vitals, an unconscious cringe.

Merlin worried them.

With a glance the old man took all this in.

Amusement beneath bushy brows. Then he looked at us, the group waiting to be shown to a table, "the witches, party of five."

Senna took a deep, slow breath and turned toward him.

"I don't believe we've met," she said. "My name is Senna Wales." She reached out a hand to shake his.

Merlin's mouth twitched in a fleeting smile. He stepped forward and took her hand. Held it. Gentle, not squeezing. Not threatening. Like a courtly old man taking any young woman's hand.

Senna's eyes drooped, lids half-closed. Merlin stared straight at her. The moment dragged on and on. Then, with a gasp, Senna pulled away.

"Don't waste your trickery on me, enchantress," Merlin said. "I was casting spells a thousand years before you were born."

Senna was shaking. She looked at her hand like it had turned into a snake. Maybe it had, at least in her eyes.

"And Merlin scores a three-pointer," Christopher commented. "That's Merlin three, Senna zip."

The gaggle of knights stirred. Someone else was coming into the room. And this time the knights didn't even pretend not to be scared.

I stood on tiptoes to see. Galahad. And looking good, I admitted to myself, looking very good, even without the armor.

Then Sir Kay moved a little to the left and I saw the person beside him.

My heart stopped beating. Literally. Beat. Beat. Pause. Silence.

The blood rushed again, eyes widened, stomach churned.

Loki.

Loki. Norse god of evil and destruction. He'd held us prisoner, chained by our wrists on the outer walls of his castle. Sent us to our deaths at the hands of his trolls. Or so he'd thought.

He was handsome, that's what was weird about him. Lustrous blond hair, high cheekbones, and perfect teeth. He could have been a model. He could have been a movie star.

He wore a green tunic with a belt encrusted with jewels, an entire jewelry store of jewels. He wore buff leggings and tall, calfskin boots. He was a Viking by way of Rodeo Drive. Perfect-fitting, perfect-looking, perfectly clean and pressed clothing, and a face to match. He looked like something carved out of marble, flawless, ageless.

"Well, screw us," David whispered.

"Loki," Senna said, but not in shock or surprise.

"Yes," Merlin said. "Loki has honored us with his presence. This should be a very interesting meal." He looked around the room, not so flip now, looked, it seemed to me, at each face in turn. And in a much lower voice said, almost to himself, "I wonder how many here will live to see another dawn."

VIII

"We've been set up!" David hissed. His hand jerked toward the hilt of Merlin's sword.

Merlin guffawed, shaken out of his gloom. "You will draw a sword in the home of Galahad? Hah-hah-hah! Here, fool, take mine. I'll have it back soon enough."

"Chill, David," I snapped. "Don't let Senna get you killed."

"Food!" Galahad yelled, oblivious to us.

Servants rushed in carrying platters piled high with meat. Whole pigs, quartered cows, slabs of mutton, a deer with everything including the head in place, mountains of quail and chickens, and some small bird that for its size and shape made me think of pigeons. Huge, crusty loaves of bread.

Bread. Ten different kinds of meat. Not a green vegetable to be seen.

"Oh, waiter, my lady friend here would like a small green salad with a balsamic vinaigrette," Christopher whispered in my ear. "And do you have any tofu?"

He made jokes with Loki right there. Loki, who had ordered us killed.

We milled toward the table. Everyone seemed to know where to sit. Everyone but us. The knights plopped down near Galahad, Merlin, and Loki, who sat together at the head of the table. They weren't happy to be near Loki. No one was happy that Loki had joined us. A fact that the god seemed to enjoy, as he smirked left and right.

We took the small chairs at one of the side tables. It reminded me of sitting at the kids' table at Thanksgiving. Except for the fact that a servant came and filled my cheap wooden cup with red wine. And except for the fact that the places where my grandparents might sit were occupied by a Knight of the Round Table, a wizard, and the Norse god of evil.

I was glad to be far away. There were a bunch of tough-looking men between me and Loki. Not enough, but better than bumping elbows with him.

I'd have been more glad to be home, my own home, my own world, far from the beautiful, evil thing that sat grinning cockily, like the one uncle who got rich.

Merlin sat to Galahad's left. Loki to his right. The place of honor.

I looked at Senna. Couldn't help it. She belonged to all this, we didn't, I didn't. How was I supposed to know what to do, how to act, who even to fear?

But Senna seemed as concerned as I was. More. A small vein in her translucent temple was throbbing. Jaw muscles clenching and releasing. Throat swallowing dust.

Remember that, I told myself, *if you ever need to act a scene combining fear with confusion and a desperate desire to gain some sort of control. Yeah, it was all an acting class. Right, April.*

Galahad and Loki, the knight and the god, were a study in male beauty. Both were handsome men. They could have been brothers. In the real world I'd have thought they were gay, far too perfect, far too perfect in the details of teeth and hair and fingernails.

But aside from the fact that either of them could have made Leo DiCaprio look like Dustin Hoffman, they had nothing in common.

Galahad was calm, assured, soft-spoken once

we were past his bellowed demand for "Food!"
His eyes were often downcast, not sad, but
thoughtful. He smiled, but not in derision, only
in welcome. He sat tall in his chair, arms held
wide, open, inviting, an equal at least in his body
language. When he spoke, he met the eyes of the
person he spoke to, listened attentively, nodded
appreciatively.

And yet there was nothing passive in him, and
certainly nothing fawning. He wasn't hoping to
make people like him. He wasn't indifferent to
their feelings, he just didn't doubt who and what
he was. He filled his space completely and
seemed almost to radiate outward, a sun at the
center of orbiting planets.

I wondered how old he was. He might have
been twenty years old. Or younger. A college junior. But, of course, that was impossible. His age,
the age of his face and features, was unreal.

And yet, put him in weathered jeans and a
baggy cotton sweater, give him a book of poetry,
and move him to a bookstore or a coffee shop,
and he could have asked me out.

Loki was very different. Restless, jumpy even,
eyes darting, mouth framing malicious smiles
that came and went with each passing thought in
his mind. He was a god, shrunken to near-human
proportions for the moment, maybe seven feet

tall. He was taller than anyone else, larger, more powerful, and yet in some undefinable way he seemed smaller than Galahad, who could not have been even six feet tall.

You could do anything to Loki, dress him in a suit and tie, or L.L. Bean flannel, or a police uniform, or a priest's cassock, and it wouldn't change the fact that you'd want to move away from him: change seats on the train, find another line to stand in, decide to walk a different direction.

"I must apologize for this poor, rustic fare," Galahad said. "I would have prepared a banquet perhaps more worthy of a god had I known you would grace us with your presence."

"Think nothing of it," Loki said. "I am a simple god."

I saw Christopher's face light up, no doubt with some joke. Thankfully, he thought it over.

The food began to be passed. Conversation picked up. The knights spoke to Galahad, he spoke to them. We, for the most part, were ignored.

"At least he's fairly normal size today," Christopher said, nodding at Loki.

Senna reached for David's hand. I got up, dragged my chair over, and shoved in between them. This brought a faint nod from Merlin.

"We have to run," Senna hissed at me.

David took a quick, appraising look around the room. "That window," he whispered. "We could jump."

"Go for it, slick," Christopher said. "That's Gala-freaking-had sitting down there. You get past him, you got Loki and Merlin. You're a bug here, man. There's no one in this room that couldn't take you down and turn you into the next rump roast."

David looked at Senna for guidance.

"Yeah, that's a good idea, ask her, she's done so well so far."

The meat was passed here and there, plates loaded, glasses filled, and everyone went to it with flashing knives and open mouths chewing, chewing, chewing.

All but me and Senna.

Galahad leaned forward and looked at me with concern. "The lady is not well?"

"What?" I squeaked. "Who, me? Oh. You mean because . . . Um, well, actually, I don't eat meat. Usually."

The knights looked a bit stunned by that stammered announcement. But Galahad only said, "You have but to command it, and if it may be found anywhere in these lands, it will be yours."

He smiled. I smiled. Okay, yes, I admit it, I was going all Harlequin suddenly. But he had a smile . . . eyes that . . .

"He didn't ask if you wanted to get married, move into a Victorian, and have three kids," Christopher said just loudly enough for half the table to hear.

"Um . . . food. Oh! Don't worry about it, your . . . Mister . . . I mean, I'm not a total vegetarian, I eat eggs and cheese, for example. I mean, it's more about cruelty to animals for me."

I am so much smoother in my mind than I am in reality.

"That's good, give him a lecture on vegetarianism," Christopher muttered. "Then you can explain —"

I kicked Christopher. He choked on a piece of ham. And Galahad yelled, "Cheese! Eggs!"

Christopher gagged, turned red, gacked out his food with the assist of a loud backslap from Jalil, and the eggs and cheese started rolling in.

They were birds' eggs, but they were hardboiled, and the bread was pretty good. The cheese was something very close to cheddar.

"Excellent mutton," Loki said. "We get too little mutton in my home country. I must arrange to have my adoring and industrious people import more sheep."

The conversations, which had gotten pretty loud, were suddenly a few points quieter. Chairs shifted. Men pulled their feet back under them, ready to move and move fast. It was like the moment in an old Western when the bad guy walks up to the saloon bar and offers to buy a drink for the good guy. And you know the good guy will refuse. And you know the bad guy is going to push it. And everyone in the bar is thinking, *How do I keep from getting shot?*

Loki's words were innocuous. Pleasant, even. But in this room of violent men, some signal had been sent that they recognized instantly.

Violence, never far away, drew very near.

Chapter IX

"I would be happy to instruct my estate manager to arrange a shipment of sheep fit for breeding," Galahad said, smiling his polite smile.

"Thank you, thank you, that's most gracious," Loki said. "And I hate to impose any further, but I'd like my witch back at the same time."

The last conversation died. Words begun were not finished. Every eye was on Galahad.

"The witch is not mine to give, Great Loki," Galahad said as he calmly stuffed a fist-sized wad of pork into his mouth.

"And yet, there she sits at your table."

"She is my guest."

Loki's polite manners were wearing thin. "Your guest is my property, Sir Galahad."

Merlin spit out a piece of gristle, swilled a

mouthful of wine, and said, "I'm curious, Great Loki. What use do you intend for the witch?"

Loki forced a smile. "What I do with my property is my concern, wizard."

Merlin nodded. "In Galahad's castle all matters are his concern."

"Don't provoke me, old meddler." Loki began to swell, to grow. Not all at once, just a little, just so that he was now twenty percent bigger than he'd been.

The consumption of meat slowed. The knights all knew exactly where their sword hilts were, exactly how many milliseconds to reach and grab and draw and swing.

Galahad raised one finger, a slight signal to his brother knights to wait.

David was eyeing a serving knife that protruded from the head of a baked wild boar.

"Perhaps we should ask the witch what she wants," Merlin said calmly, unmoved by Loki's display. "If she desires to go with you, Great Loki —"

Loki's oversized fist slammed the table, made the platters jump. Dead meat quivered. Cups spilled. Sir Gawain cursed and reached back to grab a servant for a refill.

"This is my home, Great Loki," Galahad said mildly. "You are my guest."

Loki jumped to his feet, growing still larger and more menacing. "She's mine! Mine! It was I who took her and brought her across the barrier between worlds. She is mine by right of conquest."

"You mean to use her to destroy our world," Merlin said. "That makes her every man's concern."

"Destroy?" Loki cried. "Destroy? You jackass, Everworld is already destroyed. Do you think you can withstand Ka Anor when he comes? Thor is gone. He went to battle with Ka Anor and has not been seen since. Will you stop the creature that ate *Thor* and spit out his hammer?"

Suddenly Merlin's world-weary pose dropped away. He clenched his fist and stared hard at the looming god. "I warned you, Loki. Warned you all that we could only win out if we were united. If all the gods, all the powers were united, together we could —"

"Unite? Your great dream, Merlin, a world of unity and peace, under one leader. You tried that. And where is Arthur now? Dead. Dead from your own carelessness. And yet you preach that same tired vision: Everworld united, all as one to fight Ka Anor. But I do not follow. I do not obey. I am a god!"

"It's the only way!" Merlin shouted. "Ka Anor is the god-eater, he will kill you all, one by one, and the Hetwan will exterminate all the free peoples, and that will be an end to Everworld. Together we have a chance. Viking and Greek, Mayan and Aztec and Egyptian, Celt and Briton and African, and yes, those like the Coo-Hatch who will join us, all united we can —"

"No. There is another way." Loki stabbed his finger toward Senna. "As we came to Everworld, we can return to the Old World. The thousand years of the prophecy are almost done. Leave Everworld to Ka Anor. Let the alien invaders have it. We can escape. We can escape, through her!

"I'm not greedy, Merlin. You can come, too. All the gods are welcome." He spread his hands like a misunderstood man pleading for tolerance. "Zeus's children are welcome; Quetzalcoatl and Huitzilopoctli; Isis and Osiris; and all the immortals, all welcome, all grudges forgotten. Even tiresome tree worshippers like you may come along, Merlin. A better world than this. The Old World. Just give me the witch, and we will leave Everworld and seal the door behind us."

Galahad looked up at Loki, now a giant, twelve feet tall. "The witch is my guest, Great Loki. And Merlin has his own claim to her. This is not a decision I will rush. And I will not be swayed by threats."

Loki bent down to bring his huge face, lips

drawn back in a feral snarl, close to Galahad. "They say you are the perfect knight. But I am a god. Do not oppose me. My powers are great."

"You're a long way from your home, Loki," Merlin said.

"This is going to turn bad real quick," David whispered. "All hell's gonna break loose. They'll be too busy to notice us. When it hits the fan, we book."

I didn't know if that came from Senna or from him, but either way he was right.

Loki grinned at Merlin. Focused all his malevolent attention on the old man with the bad hair. And then, suddenly, swept his arm back, caught Galahad with a backhand blow and knocked the knight out of his chair, sprawling across the floor.

CHAPTER X

The knights jumped back, drew their swords with a single ringing clang.

David lunged for the knife and yanked it from the pig. "Come on!"

Galahad rolled, wiped blood from his mouth, stood up, drew his sword, all in one fluid motion. He was suddenly a very different man. The smile was gone. The thoughtful eyes were wild, manic, excited.

Loki laughed, arrogantly sure the battle was already his.

Merlin stood apart and held up his hands as if praying. In a clear, forceful voice he said,

"Death to life,
Life to slaughter,
Arise, arise beasts of the forests,

Arise beasts of the fields,
Arise beasts of the air,
Forget your natures and become the wolf,
To kill a wolf."

And then, the wild boar, the tusked pig with its ribs stripped bare and its insides long since eaten, kicked its legs.

"Ah-ahh!" I cried.

The boar rolled over, stood on tiny hooves, and ran down the table toward Loki.

And not alone. All the dead creatures, pigs, birds, sheep, and goats all sprang to hideous life, crisp skin crackling, blackened bones rasping, empty eye sockets gaping, up they came, up from the platters, clattered over their own discarded bones and rushed at the Norse god.

A deer, gutted, meat gone from its legs, antlers cracked and charred from the fire, bounded down the table on legs of bone and tattered meat.

All these creatures rushed Loki, leaped for him, attacked him, covered his face, forced him to bat wildly at them, knocking them down only to have them jump back up.

We had frozen. The running had stopped. How could I run? How could I move? An old man had just brought dead animals to life.

But Loki was far from beaten, even as the

beasts attacked him, bit and clawed, butted and gouged, he lashed out. With one massive fist he knocked Gawain and Kay to the ground.

Galahad rushed him, sword held high, but Loki caught the sword's blade in his bare hand.

Black blood dripped from the god's hand, dripped and froze as it fell, clinking little ice cubes by the time it hit the floor.

But Loki's hand was not cut through. He roared in pain and yanked the sword and Galahad up. Galahad hung on to the sword hilt, swung back to get momentum, then forward, and slammed his feet into Loki's chest.

The god staggered under these multiple assaults. His left hand snatched and crushed the beasts, one by one, splintering them, squeezing them till their crisped fat dripped grease on the floor.

His right hand held Galahad suspended by his sword, helpless. Loki's blood dripped onto Galahad's upturned face, searing him with pain.

Perceval ran his sword into Loki's thigh, bringing a scream of pain and rage.

Merlin watched, worried, but not done yet.

> "Tree cut down,
> Tree grown old,
> Grow again,
> At Merlin's word."

The table, planks of rough lumber, came alive.
A terrifying time-lapse film, twigs shot up and
out, ripping through the tablecloth. Bright green
leaves unfurled, and branches grew at shocking
speed, warping toward Loki, branches wrapping
around his legs, entwining him in living oak.

And now the rest of the knights, recovered
from the first shock, swung into action. Their
swords hacked at Loki, careful to avoid Galahad.

Loki yanked on Galahad's sword, caused the
knight to drop free, spun the sword like the toy it
seemed to be in his massive hand, and thrust the
blade through Sir Perceval and pinned him to the
rock floor like a lab frog ready for dissection.

Blood sprayed, Perceval cried out in agony,
Galahad in horror.

David snapped out of his trance. "Now! Let's
go!"

He grabbed Senna by the arm and yanked her
away. She looked back over her shoulder, fascinated. Jalil looked sick, Christopher almost hysterical.

We ran for the door as Loki bellowed, "I will
kill you, wizard!" in a voice that shook the granite floor beneath our feet.

To the door, our backs at last turned against the
battle. Men-at-arms stood there, guards, trans-

fixed, mesmerized. But one had the presence of mind to lower his spear to block our path.

"The witch stays!" he said.

David moved fast, stepped inside the range of the spear, too close to the guard, and pressed the dirty tip of the knife against the man's throat.

"We're leaving."

"I obey my Lord Galahad."

Senna grabbed the man's hand, clenched around the spear. Pressed her hand on his and said, "This is a fight of wizards and gods, not your concern."

The guard blinked. "It's none of my concern."

David shoved him aside, yanked open the door, and we were out.

CHAPTER
XI

Down the hallway. Guards running toward us, boots thudding, swords swinging, armor clanking, running, scared, but running toward the fight, hurrying to help their master. Coming behind them, servants dragging armor and weapons for their respective knights. Like there would be time to suit up. Like there was time for anything but dying.

We brushed past them, ran some more. Not our fight. Not our problem. Not even our life or our universe. Somewhere I, the real me, was in class or at home or in the car, doing normal things. My things, from my world, not running in terror from the images of half-eaten pigs and sheep biting with heat-cracked teeth at a god who bled black ice.

"Where are we going?" Christopher demanded.

"The hell out of this castle," David said.

"Works for me," Christopher said.

A loud explosion knocked me to my knees. Flesh hit skirt hit stone. I felt pain. Ears rang. Tried to stand, confused. Looked around, everyone down, trying to stand.

The dress was torn. I noticed that irrelevant fact. My knee was bleeding. Not since I was about four had I skinned my knee. Fell off my bike. Cried. My dad comforted me. Another universe, not here.

I stood up, shaky but standing. We ran some more. Hard to run, the dress restricted me. A hallway. Another hallway. Stairs. Down and down. Yank up the dress and run, losing arm movement, balance. Where was the way out of this place?

"Left!" Jalil yelled.

"How do you know?" David demanded.

"Just go left."

Left, another hallway, a door to the right outlined with daylight.

"Through there!" Jalil yelled.

The door was locked. David yanked, Christopher yanked, kicked, cursed. We could see sunlight, and we wanted to be out in the sun.

"Hey. Excalibur," Christopher said.

For a second no one understood. Then Jalil snapped, "The knife."

We had run into the Coo-Hatch and traded them a chemistry book for a new blade on Jalil's tiny Swiss Army knife. It was made with Coo-Hatch steel. "Excalibur" was Christopher's derisive joke.

Jalil opened the blade, taking time to show exaggerated care. Coo-Hatch steel cut anything.

"The hinges," I said.

Two massive iron hinges. No ordinary blade would have made a scratch. But Jalil's Excalibur sliced through like they were made of cheese.

"Look out!"

The door fell inward. Daylight! And we ran.

Into a courtyard. Horses milled nervously in a corral. Men-at-arms gaped up at the castle keep, a massive square tower that dominated the courtyard.

The top of the tower was gone, blasted apart. The rubble was everywhere. The battle had moved. And Loki had grown. He was perhaps fifteen feet tall, more than twice the height of a man. He was injured, bleeding, black scars crisscrossing his arms and cruel, movie-star's face.

But he was not dead. Could he even be killed?

Galahad stood balanced precariously on a broken wall, one step away from a hundred-foot plunge. He stood there, unarmored, sword held in both hands, thrusting, parrying, stabbing at the towering monster.

He was bleeding red. Black hair flying in the breeze. Muscular arms strained and sweating as he fought a tireless foe.

Merlin was out of sight, but as I watched I saw a body, a body that had once been Sir Perceval, wading into the fight, sword swinging through the air. Sir Kay, too, fought though dead. He swung his sword with one hand and held his own head cradled in the crook of his other arm.

The detached head yelled soundlessly, mouth wide.

I was as cold as Loki's blood. Dead men had replaced the dead animals. Merlin's handiwork.

Christopher bared his teeth at Senna, a fierce contempt. "And you thought you'd put a spell on the guy who can do that?"

Senna was trembling. Maybe just mad. But I felt, wanted to feel, that she'd just gotten a lesson in her own weakness. A demonstration of what power meant in Everworld.

CHAPTER XII

David pointed. "The front gate. That way. There it is, through there."

Maybe he was still under Senna's spell, maybe I couldn't trust him, but he did have a way of staying focused on what mattered. He grabbed Senna and dragged her away from watching the bizarre fight.

"On foot?" I cried. "We should take the horses."

"No time," he said.

"Hurry now, but we'll go slower later," I argued, panting. "Get the horses. Otherwise they'll catch us."

David hesitated.

Senna looked right at me. "I can't ride a horse."

"Well, figure it out. I'll show you."

"David," she said, and touched his hand, "I can't ride a horse. No horse will carry me."

Suddenly I was a long way and a long time from there. I was ten. Our parents had given in to my insistent demands for riding lessons. Senna had come along, too.

First time on a horse for either of us. For me, it was the easiest, most natural thing in the world. But for Senna . . .

"I apologize, folks," the stable owner had said. "I've never seen anything like it. Even poor old Mary Belle won't seem to let your daughter near her. And Mary Belle's the gentlest mare I've ever owned."

I stared at Senna. She glared back, defiant.

"What do you mean, no horse will carry you?" Jalil said. "You can get on the horse, or you can walk."

"Find her a broom, maybe she can fly," Christopher said.

"She's telling the truth. Forget the horses," I said.

"Let's forget her instead," Jalil said.

"She says she's the only way we can get back home. We need her," I reasoned.

"Every word out of her mouth is a lie," Christopher said.

"You want to take the chance? Leave her for Loki?"

Then I saw Galahad fall. Loki's fist punched his sword arm, knocked him off balance, and sent him windmilling backward. His left foot stepped on air. He toppled.

"Good-bye, perfect knight," Loki said.

Galahad fell. But then slowed. He fell slower and slower. He turned around in midair and prepared to land gently on his feet.

Merlin, of course.

But now Galahad was out of the fight. It was wizard versus god.

"Screw the horses, time just ran out," Jalil said and led the way toward the gate.

Through the gate. Across the lowered bridge. Over the moat.

The castle was built at the edge of the sea. Intense green grass sloping down toward cliffs that crumbled into junk piles of rock. No escape there. No boat, no harbor, just the churning gray sea.

The other way there was a handful of small houses, simple but snug-looking one-story things made of mud and wood with thatched roofs.

Beyond the village were fields ripe with wheat and corn swaying in the late-morning breeze. And beyond the fields, the dark wall of the forest.

We raced across the drawbridge, over the moat, ran through the little village, oblivious to the stares, ignoring the nervous questions, running as though our lives depended on it.

There was no road, not really, just a simple path, rutted by wagon wheels that plunged through the fields toward the forest.

"Off the path, off the path," David ordered.

I turned right, into the field, running for the shelter of tall stalks of corn. Along the rows, running pigeon-toed, feet together, shoulders drawn in to fit between the stalks. My elbows banged against corncobs, leathery leaves slapped at me. A loud explosion once again echoed from the castle behind us. I paused, looked back, saw it still looming above me, gray and blackened stone between tasseled stalks.

I ran. Where were the others? I was losing them.

"David! Jalil! Christopher!"

"Right here!" Jalil yelled.

Right where? His voice was from my right. I pushed out of my row into the next one. Looked up and down. No one. Pushed through into the next row. Nothing.

I was panting, gasping for humid air thick with the smell of organic decay. My skinned knee stung. There were small cuts on my hands and arms from the leaves. Bruises on my elbows and forearms.

I wanted to cry. "Jalil? Jalil? Christopher? David?"

No answer. The sound of feet and running, but all the way back the other direction. Then, movement much closer. I pushed into the next row of corn.

Troll.

I saw its back. Like one of the great building stones of the castle had grown crude arms and legs. From behind, you couldn't even see the slung-forward rhino head. It looked like a headless thing.

I tried to stop breathing. But my lungs were screaming for air. Willed my heart to slow, but . . .

It turned.

Long blunt snout sniffed. Little pig eyes searched. Focused. It let loose a grunt and came for me.

I ran, stumbled through the row back toward the other sounds I'd heard but no, no way, I was feeble compared to the monster. I pushed the corn rows apart, the troll simply flattened them.

Loki's trolls, I thought. Oh, God, Loki had the castle surrounded. He didn't intend to lose. He'd ordered our death once before, and now, now I was left to outrun a beast that outweighed me five to one.

So tired. Run! No, think. Think! No time! Idiot, just run.

The troll wasn't fast but he wasn't tired, either. And where there was one there would be others. Where was David? And what would he do with his stupid carving knife against a troll? Huge footsteps trampled the ground, plodding, barely running, but keeping up with me. Had to lose him. *Confuse him, trolls aren't smart, April, they're stupid. Confuse him.*

Change rows. Run left. Change rows. Run right.

Suddenly, the corn was gone. No more rows! I was at the edge of a field of tall brown grass, maybe wheat, how would I know? It was almost as tall as me, but not taller. Not tall enough to hide me.

Backpack. What did I have in my backpack? Most of our pathetic worldly possessions. Keys. Was that it? Did the troll hear them jangling?

I stopped. Gasped, sucked air in a sob. Fumbled with the clasp. Keys. I snatched them in my fist and threw them.

Follow the sound, you stupid thing. Chase the sound.

Then I saw the watch. Jalil's watch. The band had been crushed and twisted. The crystal was chipped and loose, but basically intact.

Ridiculous. It would never work.

No time, April, don't be an idiot, what are you, a Girl Scout?

The corn wouldn't burn. Would the wheat?

I grabbed a handful of the dried grass and yanked hard with the strength of terror. I squatted, shaking, had to keep my hand steady. The sun beat down. Beat down on the crystal.

"Bring it to a point," I muttered, fighting hysteria. I moved the crystal, up, down, in millimeter increments. The tiny pinpoint of light grew narrower. I held it on a strand of grass.

Nothing.

The troll erupted from the corn, twenty feet away. He swung his huge head toward me. A sword was in his three-fingered hand. Then I saw the second troll. A third.

I dropped the crystal from numb fingers. No. No. They had me. I couldn't get away.

I fell to my knees. My palm landed on the crystal. I still held the handful of wheat. No other hope. Tiny, tiny hope, I had to keep trying, no other hope at all. I was sobbing. Sobbing and holding the stupid crystal, cursing and praying at the same time, blaspheming and begging for divine intercession in the same jittering sentences.

A wisp of smoke.

Blow. Not too hard. Blow.

The trolls gathered around me, all so high above me, and stared down at me with their blank, stupid eyes. Stared at the girl who was too dim to run away.

Suddenly, flame. More grass. More blowing.

Absurd. The trolls could put it out with a breath, with a foot, with a hard look, but they didn't.

The flame grew. The trolls gaped. Stared, and no longer at me. They stared at the fire, transfixed.

All at once I had a torch, a handful of burning grass. I swept the flaming grass around me in a semicircle. More grass caught fire. The trolls stepped back.

I stood up, quivering in every muscle. "That's right, I have fire. Want some?"

The breeze picked up just then and by luck, by blessed luck, it gusted the flames toward the trolls.

"Fire!" one cried.

"Yeah, and you know what Frankenstein always said: 'Fire bad!'"

CHAPTER XIII

The fire spread rapidly, too rapidly. But it made a wall of smoke and flame between me and the trolls.

I moved away from the fire, away from the trolls, keeping the warm crystal in one hand, a fistful of dry grass in the other.

I could only hope the others were away from the fire.

"I want to go home," I said, half crying. "I'm going to be in *Rent*. I'm Mimi. I have friends and family and teachers, I am not part of this, I'm not David, some wanna-be hero, just let me out of this freak show."

Talking to no one. Just needing to talk, to hear the sound of my own voice, whispered and shaky as it was. The fire was loud now, crackling almost explosively as it swept back in the direction of the castle. I was heading for the woods. Had to get out of the field, that was for sure, some idiot set it on fire.

I laughed at that, a hysterical laugh. Some idiot burned up all the flour. Bye-bye, baguette.

I reached the trees, leaned against one, closed my eyes, and took a deep breath. Then I felt the rock fingers close around my wrist.

The troll stepped from behind the tree. There were half a dozen more.

"Is that the witch?" one asked.

The one who held me leaned close and sniffed at me. "Not the witch. This one has red hair."

"Great Loki says, 'Bring me the witch.' This is not the witch."

"No," another agreed.

What must have been the leader swaggered up, full of his own importance. "This one for us."

He pushed my captor aside and grabbed me around the waist. "Mine," he said.

I hit him. I might as well have punched a bank building. He slapped me an openhanded blow that exploded lights and stars and fireworks all around me.

My vision cleared only slowly. My eyes were still swimming in sparks when I saw the lance enter the troll's right eye. It appeared over my shoulder, a spear, white wood, point planted in the troll's brain.

His horrible head began to turn to solid stone, all life, even all mockery of life draining away.

I pushed back. The arms, stiffening swiftly, moved only enough to allow me to slip down to the ground, then roll away.

The other trolls yelled and attacked. I was yelling, too, out of control, yelling, screaming, just screaming because I was face-to-face with horror and there was no rational response.

Galahad swung his sword. A troll's head dropped like a boulder. Another was cut in half. A third, punctured. Four of the seven dead within seconds.

Impossible speed. Impossible accuracy. The sword did not miss, did not miss by a millimeter. Every movement liquid, economical, so practiced, so easy it could have been choreographed.

The remaining trolls ran.

Galahad reined his horse and swept down from his saddle. He half lifted me into a classic historical-romance bodice-ripping pose, ruined only by the fact that I was bleeding, bruised, and sobbing.

"Are you hurt?" he asked.

"No," I managed. "I'm all right."

He smiled. "You roasted several trolls back in the wheat field. As a rule fair maidens remain helpless until properly rescued."

"I . . . I'm sorry. I'm not from around here."

"Mmm. It's a refreshing change. I've rescued many maidens. Never a troll-killer."

"The others. Are they . . . and Loki?"

"Your friends, and the witch, are all together. We are all together, I should say, including Magnificent Merlin. All together and fleeing. Loki has my castle, and we must make do as well as we may under the circumstances. I believe I know the place where Merlin will lead the others."

"Oh. Look, I can walk now," I said. "We should hurry. Let's get out of here."

"Ah, but you must ride," he said. "I can accept a fair maiden who kills trolls, but I cannot allow a fair maiden to refuse to share my saddle."

Galahad stood up as effortlessly as if I weighed ounces rather than pounds and swung himself and me up onto his horse. I have never been so grateful to another human being in my life.

I swallowed and blinked away tears of relief. And some strange, still-functioning corner of my mind thought, *"Share my saddle?" That's one not even Magda has ever heard.*

Chapter XIV

We didn't ride far. Not far enough for me. I felt a few hundred miles would be about the right distance to put between me and Loki. Or else an entire universe.

But Galahad found his way through forest that turned ever taller, ever darker. The underbrush became patchier, less but also more dense in places.

I tried to sit astride the horse, like a normal person would, but Galahad balked. So I sat sidesaddle. Not exactly comfortable, especially not with two in one primitive saddle. You'd think it would be romantic, or at least erotic, squeezed in close with the perfect knight. And maybe later, someday when the specific memories had faded away and all that was left was my own private myth, it would be all those things.

But right here, right now, it was the details, the reality that occupied my mind. Big details. Little ones.

Horses bounce. And getting bounced when you're resting all your weight on the one butt cheek that's on a man's thigh, while the other butt cheek just kind of hangs there in the air, so that every step sends a little impact up your tailbone and up your spine, well, that gets old fairly quickly. Not to mention the bladder factor.

Then there was the fact that despite being the finest-looking male human I'd ever seen, Galahad smelled. I couldn't blame him. He'd just come from hand-to-hand combat with Loki, followed by some more with the trolls; the man was entitled to sweat. I probably smelled, too, but the fact is I couldn't smell myself and I could smell him.

Those were the little details. The big detail was the fear.

We talked, but not much.

"Thanks for saving me."

"It is my duty. And my pleasure."

"I'm sorry about your castle. Getting wrecked and all."

"I regret the loss of it. But I have other castles. It is the villagers who suffer."

"Yeah. I guess so."

We didn't have a lot in common. He had villagers. I had a clique. But he'd just saved my life, and I wanted him to go on saving it till I was safe.

"So. Do you still have the Holy Grail?" I asked him. "I mean, you didn't sell it or anything?"

"The Grail is of the Old World," he said sadly.

"And, like, you knew King Arthur? What was he like?"

"He was a king."

He didn't ask me about myself.

Life, even in Everworld, wasn't a romance novel. I guess romance writers imagine that being rescued is a big rush, a kind of thrill that will just send you into a state of uncontrollable desire. But here I was, all alone with a shockingly handsome man who had just saved my life. A knight, no less. And mainly I just felt tired.

Fear wears you out. Real fear, not the artificial fear you get parachuting or bungee jumping. It's easy to tell the difference between the real thing and the fake: If you have any desire to yell, "Yee-hah!" it's not real.

Real fear makes you want to beg and plead and pray, *Please let me live, please, please let me live*. It makes you lose control over your own muscles, over your own mind. It makes you want to vomit.

It makes you so tired.

We rode that way, me on his lap, him scanning

the trees and the bushes, no doubt wondering how he'd fight with me on his lap.

After a while my loopy, feverish brain settled on a simple problem. *How do I tell a legend that I have to pee?* Then, just as I was thinking I'd try something Shakespearian, you know, "Prithee, milord, but I must fain squat in yon bushes, else will I dampen thy attractive knee," we were there.

We'd been moving uphill at a more and more distinct angle for some time. Up a hill that took us to the treetops and just beyond, so that I could see out across miles of forest.

Far behind us, poking up where the green stopped at the water's edge, was the smoking ruin of the castle.

We topped the long, steepening rise. The horse leaped over a low, crumbled wall, and we sauntered into a camp with striped tents going up and a big fire being built.

My friends were there. Senna, too. And Gawain and Gareth, rushing feverishly back and forth, yelling orders at the twenty or thirty men-at-arms who were doing all the real work.

Seeing them made me remember seeing Sirs Kay and Perceval. Dead and still fighting. I hoped they would somehow have a decent funeral.

Other men, some in Galahad's livery, some

working for other knights, formed a perimeter, facing out and down toward the surrounding forest.

The camp was in a sort of shallow, oblong bowl. Like a dog dish, or a tiny volcano, it had sides sloping down inward and outward from a ragged, broken lip.

I thought it must be a ruin of some sort. A tower, built atop a low hill in the middle of the forest. But the stumps of walls were covered in moss and ferns and lichen so that only the vague, suggestive outline of stones remained.

Merlin arrived at the same time we did, but coming from another direction. He looked like a man who'd just come from chemotherapy. Old. Sick. Fragile. He nearly dropped from his horse and staggered into the arms of a burly guard who dragged him into a tent.

Christopher spotted me first. "April! You okay?" he called out with real concern. "Or are you quite a bit more than okay?" he added, shifting gears into a leer.

I swung down off the horse. "Thanks for the ride, Mister . . . Sir Galahad."

He nodded absently, already focusing on Merlin. Worried. Probably he was as glad to drop me off as I was to be dropped. He was rubbing his leg where I'd been perched.

"So. Was the perfect knight a perfect late morning, early afternoon?"

"Christopher, we've got to get you a girlfriend."

"Two." He held up two fingers. "One in each universe, please."

Jalil and David joined us. Senna hung back. Fine by me. I didn't have the energy for her.

"I'm sorry we lost you," David said. "Sorry *I* lost you."

"It's not your job to look out for me, David."

He shrugged. "Yeah. Still. Sorry."

I nodded toward Senna, curious despite myself. "What's going on there?"

David looked guilty. Or embarrassed. "I think she's kind of, I don't know. Kind of stunned, maybe."

"She thought she was bad. She thought she was a player," Jalil said. "She just got a little dose of reality."

David shook his head. "You guys have it wrong. This isn't her fault. Maybe she tries too hard to control people. She's scared. She's trying to take all this crap and make it work out."

"Says the man who's sleeping with her," Christopher said dryly.

"I didn't. I mean, I don't think." He looked confused, like he was searching his memory, finding then losing what he sought. "It was like, I thought we were going to, and then, I don't know."

I could almost literally see the cynical joke building up in Christopher's brain, ready to be delivered in scathing tones.

I jumped in. "She can do that to you. Make you not believe what you've seen, or else believe what never happened."

Jalil's eyes narrowed. "One of these days, maybe when her spokesman here is away, you need to tell us what —"

David erupted. He wheeled, pushed his face close to Jalil, rose as high as he could without standing on his toes. "You got a problem with me, Jalil, you need to just say it to my face, not make snide —"

"To your face, in your face, David, I have a problem with you!" Jalil yelled, not backing down. "I don't trust you anymore. Is that straight up enough for you?"

"The witch has made you her bitch," Christopher said, barking out a harsh laugh at his own wit. "You don't be spending the night with her, and being her little sock puppet, and then come sneaking around us like we're all best buds."

David looked like he'd been ready to take Jalil on. But now it was Christopher, too. He shot a look at me, expecting me to intervene. Well, I was sick of them all. Sick of rushing around like a firewoman armed with an estrogen bucket, putting out testosterone fires.

"Kill each other, I don't care," I muttered.

"You're tired," David said. Like he was apologizing for me. He took a deep breath and made a show of reining in his anger. "Senna is one of us. From our world. Our universe. She's in our school, what do you people want?"

"'You people,'" Christopher echoed significantly.

"She's not from my universe," Jalil said. "My universe, people don't do mind-control. My universe, people don't do what April said, make you believe what isn't and disbelieve what is."

"Unless you count advertising," Christopher added.

"She lies to us, David," I said. "Uses us. I don't know how, I admit that, but she does, she is. She's using us right now, or else planning to."

He tried to go on looking mad. But it was three of us against him. And against Senna. He saw himself as our leader, and we'd just voted him out of office.

"Look, if we're going to escape from Everworld, she can help us."

Jalil snorted derisively. "Don't treat me like I'm

some kind of moron, David. You don't want to escape Everworld. You want to be Galahad, man. You want to have a castle and some boys working for you and go around killing dragons and come home to have Senna in her medieval Victoria's Secret conjuring up some ribs and cold beer. Who do you think I am, some fool who can't see you, doesn't know you?"

David didn't bother arguing with that. "You hate Senna because she's different from you, Jalil. Very enlightened. You know, some people don't like you because you're black, or me because —"

"Oh, shut up," Christopher jumped in. "Now Senna's part of the oppressed witch minority? We gotta be sensitive because she's a witch? Are you high?"

"I don't hate her," Jalil said more calmly. "Just don't trust her. Neither would you, David, except she has you whipped."

"You know what, screw you, Jalil. You, too, Christopher. You guys know nothing." David stormed off. Back to Senna. They talked, out of range of my hearing, him with his back to us. Senna watching me over David's shoulder.

The three of us exhaled all at the same time. "Great. Now it's just the three of us," Jalil said. "One less friend, one more potential enemy. Better and better."

"I don't think David is our main problem," Christopher said. "Loki's not letting us all walk away. Look at Galahad and Gawain and Gareth." He nodded toward the three knights.

Straggling groups of soldiers were arriving in the camp, some wounded. Some on stretchers. The knights were rounding them up and then sending them off into various parts of the forest. The perimeter around the crumbled walls was thinner. Men were being sent out to locate the bad guys.

I saw Galahad cast a worried look toward Merlin's tent.

"Why hasn't Loki jumped us already?" Jalil wondered.

"He's tired," I said without thinking. "Like Merlin. Both tired from the fight."

"Magic wears them out?" Jalil raised an eyebrow. "Interesting. Limits, huh? Why? I mean, magic is magic, right? We supposed to believe it burns up calories? That would make it something physical, something real. Not magic, just something that looks that way if you don't understand it."

Christopher's response was sarcasm. "Hey, I know, let's put together a discussion group. A seminar on magic. We can all discuss our pet theories. Have a speaker, break for lunch. Speaking of which . . ."

"Don't tell me you're hungry," I warned. "You saw what happened to your last meal."

"Yeah, it got up and bit Loki in the hinder. I'm still hungry. I doubt we'll be eating once Loki and his Big Uglies come tearing in here. Fighting is hungry work."

"We shouldn't be fighting, we should be out of here," Jalil said under his breath.

"I should be home. Back in the real world," I agreed bitterly.

"Yeah, well, we're not. We got Loki coming and Merlin looking like a drunk coming off three days in Mexico, and Senna and David playing Samantha and Darren. Someone make sense out of that picture."

I looked up at the trees, through the trees at the sky. It was darkening. Night would come soon. Had I been that long running? That long riding on Galahad's lap? The day seemed short. But maybe even that was in Loki's power.

"How is it getting dark already?" I asked.

Jalil shook his head like that had been bothering him, too. "How's it getting dark? How is it the weather and the vegetation say Merry Olde England when we're not two day's walk from Aztec country? How is it everyone speaks English, including Vikings and aliens? How is it dead animals get up and start chewing on guys who can

grow ten feet taller anytime they want? You want
a list of 'how comes?' I have a list a mile long."

Christopher jumped in. "How come no one
ever says, 'Those are weird shoes, man,' or 'Hey,
why is there a black guy walking around in medieval England?' or, 'What exactly is the relationship between three guys and one redhead
chick?'"

He winked at me. "I like the bra-strap look, by
the way. It makes a statement. Wonderbra?"

I was too tired to bother to tell him to go jump.
Too tired, as if the day really had passed, as if time
weren't compressed.

What time was it back in the real world? What
day?

If only I could sleep. Become me again. I'd call
Becka. She was open-minded. Believed anything,
as long as it wasn't too threatening. I'd tell her
about riding with Galahad.

"What a mess," I said, not even sure I'd spoken
out loud.

I'd thought all we needed to do was find Senna
and we could go home. Now we had her, and we
were still trapped. Trapped and divided. We'd lost
David. Not a perfect leader, but the closest thing
we had. Jalil and Christopher wouldn't follow
me, or each other.

I tried to get my mind to make sense of it all.

Save Senna or else maybe lose our one path back to the real world. But, if Loki was right, Senna was some kind of doorway for more than just us.

Loki wanted to escape Everworld as badly as I did. And once that doorway was open again, who else might go through? What other horrors?

I had stood on the steps of the great pyramid in New Tenochtitlan. I'd watched the human sacrifices climb the stairs to Huitzilopoctli's altar. Seen their hearts torn out, their bodies rolled down the stairs, blood draining . . .

Loki. Huitzilopoctli. How many other mad gods would invade our world if Senna lived?

Senna looked up at me just then. Our gazes locked. Did she know what I was thinking? Did she know that I was weighing her life, wondering which was worse: Senna alive, or Senna dead?

CHAPTER
XV

Galahad was striding toward us. I shook off a mental image of Huitzilopoctli sitting atop the Hancock Building while yuppies were hauled up by high-speed elevator to feed his blood-hunger.

I felt embarrassed by the impulse but I wanted Galahad to come and tell me what to do. Someone needed to be in charge. Someone needed to make the decisions. Didn't they? A play needs a director.

David spotted Galahad and came back, too, followed at a wary distance by Senna.

"Loki's forces will attack with the fall of his night," Galahad announced. He looked at me. "I regret that you are drawn into this, lady." He shook his head. "I should not have driven the dragon away. I should have let Merlin take the

witch then, for surely more good men will die
now to keep her from Loki."

"Let Senna go," David said at once. "Give us a
sword and food, we'll walk away, make it on our
own."

"The witch can never go free," Galahad said.
"Merlin has ordered that should the battle go
against us, she will be killed. It is a foul thing to
think on. But I am done disputing Merlin's wis-
dom. Sir Perceval, who has been my friend these
many centuries, is dead. And Kay, who was never
a friend, but was a brave companion. And others,
too. All because I could not see past my hatred of
the dragon."

It was the first sadness or deep worry I'd seen
on his face. Maybe looking scared wasn't part of
the code of chivalry. But it's not every day you
lose a friend you've had for hundreds of years.

Galahad looked right at Senna. "I do not relish
ordering your death. I would not kill a woman,
even a witch. But my archers will carry out that
order, rather than let Loki take you and carry out
his own terrible plans."

Senna instinctively took David's arm and
pulled close to him.

"Anyone goes after Senna, they have to come
through me," David said.

Galahad nodded. "You are bewitched, sir, I

know the signs well. She would make you her champion and send you into battle against me."

"I'll fight you if I have to," David acknowledged.

"I have fought hundreds, perhaps more, perhaps thousands of battles of sword against sword, lance against lance. And yet I stand." Galahad bowed slightly.

A neat, effective threat. No bragging. Just the simple statement that many had tried to kill him and he was not dead.

David tried out a tough-guy stare, but let it go when all he got back from Galahad was respectful patience. Then he said, "Look, you saved April. We owe you." He headed back to Senna.

"Gee, you must be relieved, huh? Him letting it go like that?" Christopher asked Galahad. "Whew."

If Galahad caught the joke at David's expense, he didn't show it.

"We face battle, outnumbered. We fight because it is our duty to resist evil, and because Loki's foul creatures, left to roam freely, would terrorize the peaceful farms and villages roundabout. I would be glad to have you as companions in arms. We need every strong arm. But you, all but the witch, are free to make your way," the knight said. "If that is your choice.

"I will not deceive you: Loki may win out. Merlin is weakened, drained. And without him we have no magic, only our blades. He has called to the dragons, but will they hear his voice now? And will any dragon come, where the son of Lancelot still stands?"

He shook his head. "I may have doomed us all. I have fought the dragons for so long . . . what other quest was there? What else should I have done, these many, too many years?"

"You were Lancelot's son?" Christopher said.

Galahad looked puzzled. "You speak as though I were already gone. Have you had a vision?"

Christopher seemed embarrassed, a first for him, maybe. "No, man. No. It's just . . . you know, you're history to us. Like, you happened a long time ago."

Galahad searched Christopher's face, deepening his embarrassment. Then slowly, hesitantly, he asked, "Was I real? In your world, in the Old World? Was I more than a legend, more than a tale? Was I a man?"

"I . . . I don't know," Christopher said.

"My memories are . . . I remember bits and pieces. My mother, the Lady Elaine. I remember the sword in the stone." He shook his head. "No, not Arthur's sword, another. I remember taking my seat in the Siege Perilous, the seat that would kill all pretenders but me. I know of my great quest for the Grail, though even there I am confused, for Gawain recalls the same quest, as though we were two men doing the same deed. But there are so many gaps. So many missing pieces. Perhaps I knew them once and over these too-long centuries I have simply forgotten them."

"I'm sure you were real," I said. "I'm sure you are real."

Galahad nodded and looked down at the ground. "It is a lady's right to flatter, and be flattered."

Then he squared his shoulders and shook off the pall. "Go now, if you wish, go east, quickly, and you may evade Loki's trolls and their wolves."

With that Galahad turned and walked away, instantly surrounded by men-at-arms looking for direction.

CHAPTER XVI

"Good choice," Christopher said bitterly. "Stand here and get wiped out or head off into the woods and hope that maybe, somehow, we don't run into some trolls."

"We can't leave," I said firmly. "We leave, we lose touch with Senna. She's our way back to the real world."

"You're buying that?" Jalil asked.

"I don't know," I practically yelled in sudden frustration. "I don't know anything."

Jalil thought about that, then nodded. "We have to assume it's true. For now. Till I can prove or disprove it."

"Maybe later in the lab, professor," Christopher said. "We can do a double-blind test. Then we can write it up for midterms. Hey, this is bull. Senna's the big deal around here? I don't think so. Senna's nothing. She's a pimple on Merlin's butt. And Galahad is wondering if he's real? He's real enough for me."

"It's getting dark," Jalil said.

"Yeah."

I looked at David and Senna. Mostly at Senna. The two of them were by one of the smaller fires that had been built against the encroaching night. Senna was drinking something hot, steam wafting up over her face.

"If we want Senna alive, and we're not going off on our own, we need to win this battle," I pointed out. "Better off united."

I headed purposefully toward my half sister. A faint smile flickered, her eyes darted toward me, insolent, angry.

I planted my feet a bit melodramatically, hands on hips. "There's a fight coming. Galahad isn't exactly confident. We need to stick together."

"You've decided you believe in me," Senna said.

"Believe in you? In you? No. I believe in the same God I've always believed in, and guess what, that's still not you, Senna. But maybe you're our way home, so maybe we'd better stick together. But that's just a maybe, Senna. Maybe I care whether you live or die, maybe not, so don't push it, I've had a bad day."

I looked deliberately toward the two bowmen Galahad had left standing nearby. They hadn't taken their eyes off Senna.

Senna stood up. Spread her arms. Whispered, "Come closer, April."

Firelight bronzed her pale skin. Her gray eyes shone from deep, shadowed pools. My moment of bravado was done, over.

"No."

"Are you afraid? Of me?"

Yes. I always have been. Ever since . . . "No," I lied. "Of course not."

"You want the answer to your 'maybe,' April, or are you afraid of the truth?"

I was cold. Was it cold? Was the wind blowing? I wanted to hold myself, arms across my chest, but didn't.

"Don't get near her," Christopher warned. "She wants to put a spell on you."

"I am the way home, April. And you do want to go home."

I felt strange. Felt . . . strange. The things at the edge of my vision seemed to be blurring. Darkening. And only she was touched by the light of the burning logs.

"You want to go home."

"What are you doing?" My tongue was thick. I was confused.

"Don't worry, April," she mocked. "I'm not putting a spell on you. You feel the barrier, that's all. You feel the edge. I feel it all the time."

Closer. I moved closer.

Something was happening. Something was happening to Senna herself. Her dress was growing translucent. As though the fabric was becoming more sheer. I could see her body clearly.

I shook my head, tore my gaze away to look at Christopher. He was watching me. He couldn't see what I saw.

My eyes were drawn back to Senna, and now it wasn't the dress that was translucent, but her own flesh. I could see her ribs outlined, backlit. Her heart, beating, surges of blood forced into arteries. A living X ray, ghostly, insubstantial.

My heart . . . hers. Beat. Beat.

The ribs and heart and veins were clear now, too, as though made out of glass. Then even the outline of glass faded and was replaced by a strange light, curtains parting . . .

I was flying. Floating. Weightless, drawn toward her, unable to resist, all will gone, mind numb, body hands legs all so far away.

Floating toward the parting curtain. Into the light. Not the light I expected, not celestial, not heavenly, not a glow that filled me up with hope.

A hard, harsh light. Flat. Tinged with blue.

I reached. Hands outstretched to the light. Then, I smelled something. Flowers? No. Not quite. Not so true, not so fresh.

Soap.

My head went through the gap, into the light.

I saw white tile. Sink. Toilet. Glaring, harsh light.

My bathroom. In the real world. In my home.

I saw the mirror. My reflection. A head and two hands reaching out of nothingness.

I screamed.

Senna laughed, the sound was inside me.

I fell back, reeled, hit something yielding. Felt arms take hold of me, screamed again, and fought against the arms in blind panic.

"It's me, it's me, chill, it's okay." Christopher. His arms.

He pushed me upright. Awkward, trying not to offend.

I stood away from him and realized my face was bathed in sweat, my hair matted down on my forehead.

Senna was Senna again. Whole. Opaque. Solid.

"So much for 'maybe,'" she said.

"Here they come!" a voice cried.

And from the forest below, down in the dark, came the bellowing roars of the trolls.

CHAPTER
XVII

"You disappeared into her body," Jalil said tersely. "The upper part of your body just kind of merged into her. Your body, your legs and butt and all were just sticking out of her."

He sounded weird. Easy to understand.

"I was in my bathroom," I said with a far-off voice belonging to someone else. "Back home. Like I was floating out of the shower."

"It's over that way," David said, nodding across the camp. "That's where they're coming from. That direction."

He was jumpy, ready to go. His hands were grasping for weapons he didn't have. He was avoiding looking at Senna. I saw it all, too clearly.

"First things first, we stay alive, that's first," Christopher said.

All of it swirling around me. Unreal. The fire,

the faces, the black trees over us. The sound of iron and steel clashing in the near distance, the running men-at-arms, the horses neighing nervously. Reality, but reality the way it is when you've got a hundred and four temperature and things are real but outlined with a glow; real but not as real as they should be, not quite right.

I had traveled through Senna's body. From one universe to another. From here to a fluorescent white tile artifact of an entirely different reality.

And now here I was again, danger rushing toward me, death so nearby and all I could think of was that I had smelled the soap, smelled the traces of perfume, all but touched the clean, cool, solid reality I'd always known.

The bitter reality: It was true. Senna was the way home. Senna had all the power now. All the control. It was all her.

And yet she didn't look powerful. She looked haunted. She kept flinching, shying away from the sound of battle. This was a fight to control her. Loki or Merlin. Either way, she lost.

"You feel the edge," she'd said. *"I feel it all the time."*

"Look at this camp," David said angrily. "No entrenchments, no breastworks, no defenses at all. Shouldn't these guys have spread evenly around? There should be a reserve, ready to throw in where they hit. Galahad may be the perfect knight but he sucks as a general. Sitting ducks. They can overrun the camp."

"Then stop whining and do something, General," Senna snapped impatiently.

David looked like he'd been slapped.

"Protect me. Stop them. Go! Go! You swore to save me."

"But I . . . it's too late to . . ." He looked at me, like I could help. Then a light went on in his eyes. "Jalil. Give me Excalibur."

"What?"

"The knife. The stupid knife."

Jalil fished it out of his pocket. There was a savage roar from the invisible battle. Human voices in triumph. Maybe it would be all right after all. Maybe Galahad and Gawain were pushing them back. Maybe we were saved.

"If they break through they'll come from there," David said. "Galahad and his boys first, backing up, then the trolls. Up the incline." He ran to the wall and jumped atop the green-grown stone. "See? Well, you can't see it very well in the dark but there's high ground there and there, leading down from here. It will funnel them this way. We need to break them up."

"How?"

"Trees. We drop some trees."

"Let's go!" Jalil said. "If we're going to block their path we want to do it farther down the incline."

"Not block," David said. "We block them, they're used to that. They know about climbing walls. Trolls, man, they'll go over the trees or shove them aside. We can't stop them, we have to break 'em up. Kill them. Kill more of them than they can afford to lose. Instead of laying trees across their path, we drop the trees this way."

He demonstrated with his hands. "The battle is at point A, we're point B. We drop the trees in that same line. The trolls come this way, like traffic up the interstate. We divide them. Like toll booths. Break them up into lanes. The branches are intertwined, that slows them down. And our guys are on the trees, shooting down at them."

He sprang into action, with Jalil and Christopher right behind him. I stayed back to talk to Senna. I grabbed her arm, then let it go. I was afraid to touch her. Afraid of what she was.

"If you're holding anything back, Senna, if you're playing games with their lives, you better know: There are things that matter more to me than getting home."

Having delivered my lame little threat like a badly written exit line, I took off after the others.

The Coo-Hatch steel sliced easily through the

tree bark. But the blade was less than two inches long and the first tree was three feet in diameter.

It took forever. And the roars of human victory had given way more and more to the bellowing of trolls, joined, chillingly, by the howls of wolves.

I had the horrible feeling that I had cheated the trolls once already and could not a second time. I had defied probability. Probability wouldn't let me do it again.

"There it goes," Christopher yelled. "I mean, tim-ber!"

The tree angled, snapping the remnants of its trunk, gathered speed, falling into darkness, landing at last with a thump and a crunch and the rustling of leaves.

"Okay, now that one," David said, and we ran.

It was exhausting. Swinging the tiny blade back and forth, slice and slice. Cutting wedges from the living tree. A tiny wedge, a larger one, incremental, nerve-racking progress. When one tired another took over. David paced along the low ridge, back and forth, surveying the ground as well as he could in near-total darkness. Looking back up to the camp, down to the sound of battle.

It was chilly but not cold enough to keep the sweat from forming and running in freezing rivulets down my back and temples and chest.

The trolls. What would they do? What would they do to me? When he had taken my arm, those stone fingers, when I'd felt the irresistible strength, realized my own puniness, my own . . . What would they do?

The clash of swords grew nearer. Howls of pain, human and troll, like the music of madness. The wolves, more numerous all the time. So close, those howling, mocking voices, those snarls and barks. Were they participants? Or only interested spectators, waiting for a feast?

We were without weapons. Playing lumberjacks in the dark, waiting for the rock-hewn monsters to appear out of nowhere and tear us apart.

Where was Galahad? Where was Merlin?

Another tree dropped. Not as neatly as we wanted, but it formed a channel just fifteen feet wide.

A third tree, and a second channel, this one twenty-five-feet wide at the far end, less as it came closer to camp. The channels were choked with interlocking branches, shivered saplings, standing trees. An obstacle course whose complexity was not immediately apparent.

I heard cries so close they might have been my friends. Darkness was near-total.

A fourth tree. Crash. Tim-ber. All of us panting,

but at least we were doing something. Something.

"Everyone. Out to the ends. Pick a tree. Guide them when they come." David was bent almost double, gasping for breath. "I have to go to camp. Be back."

Off to find Senna, no doubt. I couldn't be angry. If we had a hope at all, it had come from David.

I ran. Out along the tree trunk, slipping, careful! If I fell off, broke a leg, twisted an ankle, the battle would roll over me. The trolls would find me. Impossible to put the horrors out of my mind, the curse of a good imagination.

What did trolls do to women they caught? What did wolves do to anyone? When I was ten I held a bake sale to raise money for the project to return wolves to Yellowstone.

Maybe I could tell the wolves that.

I saw faint flashes in the gloom. Armor. Swords. They were all fighting blind. Could the trolls see in the dark? Of course, yes, all the stories had them living under bridges.

Madness! There were no such things as trolls. No such thing as Loki, no lunatic gods who craved human blood.

I pushed as far as I could, into the branches

that poked my eyes and sawed at my bare arms. It was like climbing a tree without regard to gravity. I wrapped my arms around a branch that should have been horizontal. I leaned against it, closed my eyes, oh, sleep, if only I could sleep and go away.

Close. Clashing swords. Exhausted grunts. Sobs of pain and frustration. And then, I saw him.

His black hair was lank, his shoulders hunched, but Galahad's sword flew, back and forth, as if he'd just stepped out onto the field. Three trolls pressed him close, swinging their own swords and massive clubs, beating at him, assaulting him with sheer violence, the sheer weight of violence.

He had to fall. But he did not. Step by step they drove him back. His men formed a line to the left and right of him. A thin line, a short line, and the trolls crowded around, trying to turn the line, get behind them, cut them off and finish the slaughter.

"Mr. Galahad," I yelled. "Galahad! There are trees behind you. We cut them down. Come back this way. Keep coming back."

Footsteps. Boots on wood.

Behind me. No!

I turned. Slipped, grabbed a second branch,

and held on, cantilevered precariously out from the tree.

Not a troll. One of Galahad's men, one of the reserves from the camp. David had brought them.

"Excuse me, my lady," he said tersely.

He fitted an arrow into his bow, drew it taut, and let fly. The arrow passed over Galahad's shoulder and went straight into the neck of a troll.

At last Galahad realized what was happening. "Fall back," he cried. "Fall back."

The knights and their men fell back into the narrow channels formed by the trees. And the trolls, unled, ungeneraled, followed.

Archers crowded onto the tree trunks and poured arrow after arrow into the compressed, immobilized mass of trolls.

Once again, it was human voices raised in triumphant cry. But far fewer than before. Far fewer.

I ran. Without a weapon I was useless, a body in the way. I ran, and felt like a coward.

CHAPTER
XVIII

Merlin still lay in his tent. And now Galahad was carried there, pale from loss of blood.

I followed him. David, Jalil, and Christopher did, too. David had not reunited with Senna. Whether that was deliberate or accidental, I didn't know.

I hadn't seen my half sister since the battle in the trees. I didn't want to see her. I no longer guessed about Senna, I knew. She was something different from me. Greater than me.

Galahad was on a pallet on the floor. Gawain knelt by his head. Merlin was on his knees, grinding something in a mortar and pestle. A servant was stripping Galahad's clothing. He was cut in more places than I could count. But the major wound was a gash across his stomach, just below the navel. Someone had wrapped a dirty cloth around his midriff but the cloth was saturated with blood to the point where blood was pooling on the dirt floor.

"Don't waste your time with me," Galahad said to Gawain. "The men need you."

"The enemy has fallen back," Gawain said, blotting his friend's sweating forehead with a scarf. "They will not attack again before Loki comes."

"And when Loki comes, not even Gawain will be able to stop him," Merlin muttered.

Galahad took the wizard's hand. "I fear I have destroyed all your plans, Merlin. Had I let the dragon —" He seized, shuddering from the pain and loss of blood.

"Stop the bleeding," I said. "He's going to die unless you stop the bleeding."

Galahad tried to focus on me but failed to find me. "Death is already perched on my shoulder. I have lived a long, long life. More than any —"

Again came the tremor that shook him from head to toe.

"Look, he's not dead yet. Stop the bleeding," I said.

"You have done well, my lady, fought valiantly," Merlin grumbled, "as have you all. I am preparing a potion that will ease his suffering. But no power can save this good knight now. His blood has run out."

"Well, you can try," Jalil snapped. "Sew up the wound at least."

"Transfusion," I said. "We could . . . okay, I mean, we would need a hollow needle. Two. And some kind of tube."

Merlin was focused on Galahad's face and absently grinding his powder, but he glanced up nevertheless. An interested look. In the midst of the madness, Merlin was still intrigued by something new.

"What is this transfusion?"

"Take blood from one person, a healthy person, put it in someone who's bled too much. But you'd need hollow needles. Never mind. Sorry."

It was true, most likely. Merlin had seen many wounds. And the blood was everywhere. Everywhere except in Galahad.

"The pens," Jalil said suddenly. "The pens in your pack. Get them out."

I whipped off my backpack, having absolutely no idea what Jalil was up to. I pulled out the pens and handed them to him. One was a click-style. The other was your basic Bic.

Jalil pulled out the ink cartridge. A hollow, plastic tube. He held it up for me to see.

"No way," Christopher said.

"Way," I snapped. "I'm type O. Universal donor. We need to boil the cartridge, get the ink out of it. Also boiled rags to clean up his wounds."

"On it," Jalil said and ran.

I pushed forward and knelt down beside Galahad. I don't know what I thought I was doing. I had about as much medical knowledge as any average person on the street. Not much. Although maybe it was a lot compared to the average citizen in Everworld.

"Get me a needle and thread."

"I can sew up a wound, girl," Merlin said.

"Wash your hands. In . . . um, wine, I guess. The alcohol will help a little."

He stared hard, annoyed I guess by some girl snapping out orders. But he was curious, too. And maybe he sensed I wasn't just making things up. Curiosity beat out ego. He washed his hands carefully in a stream of red wine poured by Sir Gareth.

"David, open the Advil. Someone get a drink for Galahad, no, no, not wine, for crying out loud, water."

"Use the wine," David interrupted. "Who knows how clean the water is."

"Okay, try, like, okay, um, four Advil," I said. I shook them out into my hand and pressed my palm against Galahad's lips. His face was burning up. Fever. Well, the Advil would help that. And might do something against the pain. Did wonders for cramps. Of course cramps weren't twelve-inch gashes across the belly.

"Dr. Quinn, Medicine Woman," Christopher said under his breath. Then added, "Let me know if I can help."

"Get some light. Can't see anything in here."

Merlin began to unwind the cloth wrapping.

"Christopher and David, wash up," I ordered. "And then order a chem seven and a CBC, type and match, stat. Where's Noah Wylie when you need him? Sorry, I'm babbling."

"What is the meaning of the washing?" Merlin asked.

I'd almost forgotten him. He was staring at me from beneath his bushy brows, half suspicious, yet fascinated, a needle in his hand, threaded, ready.

"Gets rid of the germs." Yeah, that explained a lot. "Um, see, diseases and infections and all are caused by germs. They're tiny little animals, so small you can't see them. You wash them off the wound and off anything that touches the wound. Like your hands. Speaking of which."

I grabbed a bottle of wine and bathed my

hands with it. Probably not enough alcohol in wine to do much good, but it couldn't hurt.

Jalil came racing back in. He held the now-clean plastic tube.

"Okay. Here's what we do. Jalil, hand me one rag. Christopher and David? I want you to apply direct pressure with the palms of your hands."

"On the blood?" David asked, aghast.

"No, on his ears, David. Of course on the wound. Direct pressure to slow the bleeding while Merlin is sewing. Not much point putting blood in him if it's just going to run back out, just do it, just freaking do it! Okay. How are you doing, Mister Galahad?"

"I endure this so that I may be returned to battle," he said. "But I cannot endure talking to a woman so embarrassingly situated."

"Embarrassingly . . . oh, please. That's the least of your problems." I actually smiled. More worried about his modesty than staying alive. "Idiot. If women were like that we'd never have any babies."

"I don't think you should call the patient an idiot," Jalil said.

"Oh, my God. Did I say that out loud? Sorry. Really. Okay, get ready. Now. No, left a little, David, on the wound, on the cut."

Direct pressure reduced the bleeding. Either

that or Galahad was running out of blood. There didn't seem to be any major arteries cut. It was more of a steady seepage than a gush.

Merlin began to sew. He did it with expert ease, showing the economical moves of someone who had done this often before.

At least he knew what he was doing. A thousand times more than could be said for me.

"Artery to vein," Jalil said.

"What?"

"We have to put it in your artery, his vein. Right? I mean, we want the pressure to force it out of you and into him."

"How do you know?"

"Know? Know? I don't know anything. It makes sense is all. No, wait. Vein to vein. Don't mess with arteries."

"How do you tell one from the other, anyway?" Christopher asked.

Good question.

I took a steaming, painfully hot rag and washed my arm, the crook of my elbow.

"I need a tourniquet. Unbelievable, I'm getting my medical knowledge from *Rent*. Mimi's a junkie. I need to make the veins pop up to find them."

David whipped off his belt and tightened it around my arm.

I took a couple of deep breaths. Nothing to do

now but stick a plastic tube, an ink cartridge, for God's sake, into my arm.

"Jalil?" I begged.

"Oh, man. Oh, man." He knelt beside me. "Okay. Okay. April? Don't move." He pressed the tip of his knife ever so slightly against a throbbing cord in my arm.

"Yah!"

Blood sprayed him in the face. He jerked back. I pressed my index finger down on the tiny cut. The tourniquet had slowed but not stilled the rush of my blood.

"Okay, I'm cool," Jalil said.

"Glad someone is," Christopher said.

"Put the tube in. I'll hold it," I said quietly.

"Like drilling for oil, man, we got a gusher."

"Just do it!" I snapped at no one.

Jalil slid the end of the tube under my index finger and into the vein or artery or whatever it was. A fine spray of blood shot from the other end. Jalil topped it with his thumb. The tube jabbed me, not so much a pain as a hideous feeling of something being very wrong.

Merlin was almost done sewing. He looked up after each suture, utterly fascinated.

I moved, with exaggerated care, with Jalil shadowing me, to sit next to Galahad. David had already tourniqueted his arm.

"Okay, dude, probably not your biggest injury ever, but hold still," Jalil instructed the knight. He found what we all hoped was a vein.

The short tube now connected us, Galahad and me. My blood into him.

"I'll take his tourniquet off first," David said. Then, "Okay, now yours."

Blood shot from the hole, sprayed and ran out around the tube. But it also went through the tube. Six fingers from three different people stanched the leakage. And now the transfusion was under way.

"I will have a woman's blood in my veins, in my heart," Galahad grumbled. "I will no longer be a man."

"Yeah, that's pretty much how it works," I snapped. "You get female blood and your willie falls off."

He looked worried. So did Merlin.

"It's a joke," Jalil said. "Blood is blood, not male or female or black or white. It's divided into types, but not the way you think."

"How long should we go on with this?" Christopher asked.

"Um, okay, let's see, diameter of the tube, rate of flow," Jalil began, then gave up.

"Do it till I start feeling faint," I said.

We held our positions, aching, straining, for an

hour. Merlin never moved, never wavered in his attention. He was witnessing a miracle. Better: Something he could do himself, someday.

Then at last Jalil said, "Okay, that's gotta be enough, right?"

I pulled out the tube. I bandaged my elbow with freshly boiled rags. At last, I stood up, drew a deep breath, felt the blood rush from my head, dropped the hymnbook from my hand and yelled, "Oh, dammit, I can't take this anymore!"

The priest stared.

About a hundred and seventy-five people stared.

The choir stared.

"Sorry," I whispered and buried my head. Then I added, "Really sorry."

My parents had the pained expressions of people who are determined not to notice something that cannot possibly be ignored.

A few old biddies made shushing noises.

Church. I was at Mass. I looked down at my arm. No wound. No puncture hole. No dried blood.

Good thing I hadn't yelled anything worse. The priest was blushing. He was young. Probably thought I was making a comment on him. A bad review from the fifth pew back.

I must have passed out. The blood loss, the exhaustion. But I was back in my own world. Friends seated nearby. My folks. The cross. The hard, uncomfortable "stay awake" wooden pew.

Let it last. Let it go on. Only don't let the trolls come while I'm asleep, don't let their faces be what I saw when I reawoke.

Don't let —

I was back and Merlin himself was holding a cool rag to my face.

"You fainted," he said.

"Yeah. I . . ." I looked around. Galahad was lying on his pallet to my left. He was unconscious, or asleep. Not moving, but breathing heavily.

"When you fell, your spirit left you. I took you for dead. Then I felt your pulse and found that life was still in you."

I sat up. He pushed me back again. "I am a poor physician, but I do understand the need for rest," he said gently.

Jalil's face hovered into view. "You okay?"

"Yeah. I popped in and out of church. Woke everyone up, that's for sure."

He nodded. "Gawain says it's about to start up again. David and Christopher are already out there. They need anyone who can swing a sword. I'm going. Just wanted to make sure you were okay first."

I took his hand, making him acutely uncomfortable. He held my hand like he wanted to put it down and didn't quite know where he should put it.

"Jalil, you guys shouldn't . . . I mean, be careful."

"Nothing to worry about," he said with grim humor. "Just a pissed-off god of destruction and a few hundred trolls in a forest at night."

"We have to give up Senna," I said suddenly. "It's the only way. Let Loki take her." I looked at Merlin. The sympathy in his eyes faded. He wasn't going to give up Senna. To my surprise, neither was Jalil.

"Give up Senna and what, have this crowd show up back in the world?"

"Yes," I urged. "The world has dealt with all kinds of psycho killers. Loki will be just one more."

"Yeah? Maybe you're right. Then again, there are a lot of superstitious, vulnerable minds back there in the world," he said.

It occurred to me he meant me, as well as anyone. I knew Jalil's beliefs, or lack of them.

"People believe anything," he said. "Y2K has brought them out of the woodwork. No one's going to drop it just because we're off by a year or so, these characters, bunch of gods, bunch of immortals start unloading in the Chicago suburbs, how long before they have a million followers each, all yelling about the end of the world and ready to make it happen? Huitzilopoctli marching human sacrifices into camps or whatever? We live in a superstitious age. People's heads full of mush. Heads full of mush and now I have to go save their sorry, stupid butts."

He shook his head. "Not that I'm bitter or anything."

From outside the tent came the sound of shouting. A brave rallying cry.

"Don't worry," Jalil said with a glance at the unconscious Galahad and a more penetrating glare at Merlin, "we still have Gawain."

He dropped my hand, turned, and walked quickly out of the tent.

"Can't you do anything?" I asked Merlin.

The old man sighed. "Perhaps. Soon. Not yet. I have called for help, but it may not arrive in time, or may refuse altogether. Dragons are not fond of Galahad. He has killed so many over the centuries. Had he died . . . but he lives."

I looked at the pale young face of the perfect knight. "You say centuries. How old is he? He seems young."

"He will seem unchanged forever. But he came to Everworld many hundreds of years ago. Back when the barrier was less strong. Him and the others. And me. We came together. We were, after all, creatures of myth and legend. When the gods made Everworld they drew with them all creatures touched by magic. Some appeared here from the first. Others came over time."

I sat up. This time he let me. "I don't belong here. None of us does."

"No. You were carried here by happenstance. You were tied to the witch. She summoned you, knowing what might happen. And the disturbance wrought by Fenrir at Loki's command carried you here."

"Not all the way here," I said. "When we sleep, we reappear in our own world. There's another me. Me, I mean, the real me. Whatever. The other me is over there, living my life. And when we lose consciousness here, we're there. It just happened again."

Merlin nodded, like that was interesting all right, but not the weirdest thing he'd ever heard. "I felt the spirit leave you. That would explain it." Then he smiled. "I would give much to see your world."

"My world?" I almost laughed. "I don't know. It's pretty different. Not a lot of magic there. Not your magic, anyway."

"Tell me. What has changed since the days of Arthur and Lancelot and Galahad? And Merlin?"

"Everything." It was too big a question. What hadn't changed? People, maybe. "We have cars. Like, um, wagons or whatever, only they go without horses. Trains. Planes. Planes are flying machines. Internet. Books."

I shook my head. What could I tell him? It was insane. The enemy was coming, my friends might be going to their deaths, my life was madness, and I had to try and summarize the last thousand years of human history in a pop quiz.

"Have you learned the secret of turning lead into gold?"

"Say what?"

"Lead into gold. Have you learned the great secret, uncovered the Philosopher's Stone?"

Galloping hooves. The men were leaving to confront the advancing trolls. David, Christopher, and Jalil with them. I felt like a traitor. It was my fight as much as theirs. Just because I was female didn't exempt me.

I tried to stand up. Merlin held me back. "No. Your arm has not the strength to wield a sword that would cut down a troll."

"Don't give me that 'upper body strength' stuff. I can try."

I walked, shaky, out into the night. A concussion. A fainting spell. A quart or two low on blood. *Lucky I could walk at all,* I thought. I saw the horses and running men on foot pulling out of camp.

I couldn't catch up. But I had to do something. I spotted Senna, standing with her two guards by the fire. I ran-staggered over to her.

"You're supposed to have some kind of powers, or whatever. Can't you do anything?"

"Like put a spell on Loki? Sorry. Little out of my league."

"If they lose, Loki gets you."

She rolled her eyes. "You know, I think that may have occurred to me, April. Yeah, I'm pretty sure that very thought has crossed my mind. And if they win, Merlin locks me in a tower somewhere till I die of old age. Wow, aren't I just the popular one?"

A sudden roar of voices made us both jump. Too close. The battle, out of sight, but within hearing. This time the felled trees would not confuse the trolls. They would drive Gawain and the others back. And then, with the backbone of resistance broken, Loki would arrive.

That's what Merlin's waiting for, I realized. He's saving his strength for Loki. But that wouldn't help my friends.

"Why did you drag us here?!" I demanded bitterly.

Senna thought it over. Then she said, "It's a dangerous world here. I understood too little. Just knew it was going to happen. I didn't . . ." She shook her head and looked away. But not before I saw the sadness on her face.

"Didn't what?" I pressed.

"I didn't want to be alone. Pathetic. And I needed a champion."

"David?"

"All I could find on short notice."

It made me mad, the way she said that. Maybe David wasn't Galahad, exactly, but he was risking his life for her, for me. For the world.

All she could find on short notice?

"What did you think it was going to be like here?" I demanded. "I mean, how much did you know? Did you know you were going to someplace full of dragons and trolls? Did you know about Loki?"

"We're not friends, you and me, April. Don't stand there hating me and still trying to pump me for information, okay?"

I could have slapped her. But there was no way of knowing what she could have done to me in return.

Sudden, renewed shouting. We both started. So

close. And then, the first heads appeared over the lip of the clearing. Human heads. I saw Sir Gareth. I saw Christopher.

"Curtain up. Final act, right, April?" Senna said. "Break a leg. That's what you're supposed to say, right? You get to play the part of the girl who entertains the trolls."

The men were backing up, running. They and ten or fifteen others all vaulted over the low wall, turned and prepared to meet their pursuers.

More men. Then Jalil and David, almost together. David stumbled, more from exhaustion it seemed to me than anything else. He took a while getting back up. But then he joined the others at the low ramparts.

Gawain was the last to come over the crumbled green wall.

An instant later the trolls were there, looming up, just past the pathetically thin defensive line.

"I have to go," I said.

CHAPTER
XXX

I had no weapon. Didn't matter. Someone would fall, someone would die and drop a sword for me.

What was I saying? A sword? What did I know about swords? What did I know about fighting and killing? I could die. Anyone could do that. But could I kill? Even an inhuman troll?

Did I have a choice? I wasn't some helpless female from a 1950's horror movie. I wasn't Fay Wray, screaming again and again as King Kong lifted me up. I believed in equality. I believed that women should be allowed in combat. I believed, I believed all the good feminist stuff I should believe. I was Sigourney Weaver.

But I was so afraid.

So are they, I told myself. *So are David and Christopher and Jalil.*

The men didn't want to die, either. But they didn't feel like they had a choice. They had to fight. They'd been raised from birth with the understanding that the day might come when they would have to go to war.

And for me, for all women, it wasn't that way. I had never played the video games, the mock battles, never run the fantasies through my head, never channel-surfed and felt the draw to stop at every battle scene.

"So? Going off to war?" Senna mocked me.

I hadn't moved. I was still standing there, and the trolls were pushing their way up the slope, up against the scared, scarred, shouting, gasping men. Soon the line would collapse. Soon the trolls would rush and crush and drive the men before them and pour in on us and what was I going to do, stand there and scream, "Save me, save me" when there was no one left alive to save me?

I started walking. Knees locked. Stiff. Forcing my body to move, and then seeing, as though from far off, that movement had become automatic. Forward. Closer. No longer even involved with the act of moving, the choice made, now could not be unmade.

A roar of triumph as Sir Gareth's head was knocked from his shoulders. It rolled. A croquet ball on the grass. A basketball that has bounced off the court. I should pick it up and throw it back, that would be the polite thing to do, pick it up and throw it back so the boys could go on with their game and —

One of the men-at-arms staggered toward me, running like he had something to give me or show me, running, then he dropped. Dead of no visible wound, just dead.

His sword lay in the grass.

I picked it up. The handle, the whatever they called it, the hilt, yeah, it was wet, wet with blood. Slick leather bound with some kind of cord for easy gripping. It was heavy. Three, four, five pounds? It felt like more.

The line broke. David was being driven back, separated from Gawain, the line broke and the trolls rushed in, rushed straight at me.

David hacked. A troll fell. Too many more to take his place, all rushing, all coming for me.

Straight for me. Helpless female. Time to run and trip and scream, "Save me!"

But I couldn't move. Not my feet, not the sword. I just stood there, frozen, sword held point downward. Paralyzed.

And the troll in the lead hesitated. Slowed. Stopped, ten feet away from me, staring at me, uncertain.

Time stopped. He sniffed at me, like a wild

animal, suspicious. And I stared at him, emotion
all too far away to touch me.

I heard a rustling sound behind me.

Saw the troll's little pig eyes look past me.

"Oh, good," Galahad said airily. "The battle isn't
over just yet."

That broke the spell. I turned, looked, and yes,
he was there. Pale but unwavering. His bare chest
a mess of unhealed wounds and smeared blood.
The Frankenstein stitches across his lower belly
were a hideous grin.

In the weird silence he said, "My lady, I would
not intrude if you are determined to stain your
sword with this troll's blood. But if not, I beg you
to do me the honor of letting me kill him for
you."

I said nothing. The trolls gaped. And then
Christopher yelled, "Galahad!"

He nudged David and David echoed the cry.
"Galahad!"

One by one, then in twos and threes, the bat-
tered men-at-arms began to take up the chant.
"Galahad! Galahad!"

The trolls quailed, and the men attacked, still
crying, "Galahad!"

The perfect knight watched, nodding approval,
resting his weight on his sword as if nothing here
yet required his help.

He couldn't do any more. It had taken all his strength to walk out of the tent and put on that brave display.

The trolls fell back, retreating from the camp, over the wall. But the men did not have the strength to follow them. Most collapsed on the ground, panting, groaning, begging someone, anyone for water.

I went to Galahad.

"You shouldn't be up," I said.

"And you should not be standing alone against an onslaught," he countered.

I shook my head. "I wasn't. I just froze. Couldn't move."

I realized it must have looked as if I were being brave. I must have looked as though I were standing there like a rock, just me and my borrowed sword, ready for anything the trolls had.

Not exactly the truth.

"I feared that having your blood flowing in my veins would unman me," Galahad said with a shadow of his old smile. "Now I see that it can only make me more bold."

I didn't know what to say to that. It wasn't the kind of compliment you hear very often. A perfect knight doesn't come up every day and compliment me on my blood.

"Oh." I said. "Thanks."

I'd been wrong. Sometimes fear did leave you with a sense of "go for it." Maybe I was getting used to being scared. Maybe there were different varieties of scared. Maybe I was somewhere past being scared, or just losing my mind, but part of me badly wanted him to lift me up onto his horse and ride away to some castle, or at least some Marriott.

He was a babe. Better, he was a man. He was a man that other men thought was a man. Sir Gawain had yelled his name like all the others. And here I was, the only non-witch woman within miles. And we were probably going to die. He would die, and my friends, and I'd have to die without even having him kiss me, which seemed a hell of a waste, except that how do you smoothly move the conversation from "nice troll-killing" to "shut up and kiss me before we get killed"?

Senna would have been able to —

Senna. Stop the tape.

Where was Senna?

As if in answer, a huge, familiar voice, a voice that bent the trees with a terrific wind, roared, "I have come for my witch!"

CHAPTER
XXI

The men dragged themselves up to their feet. David, Jalil, and Christopher came trotting back to me and Galahad. Jalil had a mean little cut under one eye. A gash of white fat and red blood.

"Where is she?" David demanded of Galahad.

Galahad looked around, as unsure as I was. No Senna.

"Where is she?" David repeated, frantic. "He's coming. Loki is coming."

Something large was crushing through the underbrush just out of sight, pushing the trees aside, shaking the earth with the weight of each step.

King Kong after all.

It occurred to me in the rational, observing quarter of my mind that Loki understood theatrics. He was building the fear. Building the dread. Using suspense as a weapon. Like a good director.

"I do not know," Galahad said, troubled. He called to the men who'd been guarding her. "What of the witch?"

They seemed puzzled. As if the question were slightly embarrassing for Galahad. "My lord, you sent word she was to be released."

"Sent word?!" he snapped. "Who gave you this message?"

It was immediately apparent from the blank looks that neither man actually remembered getting that message.

Senna had planted the suggestion.

"You have been bewitched," Galahad said. "Go, men. Join the others."

Now it was the trolls chanting, their own brutish echo of our own voices.

"Loki! Loki!"

"She took off," Christopher said bitterly. "Big surprise."

"At least we can stop this stupid battle," I said. "Loki just wants her. We can just tell him."

"Like he's going to believe us?"

"He'll believe Galahad," I pointed out.

"Better she be free than in Loki's hands," Galahad said.

David nodded. "We have to distract Loki. Keep him fighting. Otherwise he'll send his trolls after her."

Galahad shook his head slowly. "We pay a fearful price for my ancient hatred of dragons. The witch might now be safe in Merlin's care, far from here, in some enchanted place only Merlin knows."

Jalil touched the wound by his eye. Winced at the pain, and at the unfamiliar feeling of parted flesh. "You know, Sir Galahad, you could have just killed Senna. Solved everyone's problem at once. Except ours, of course. End of issue."

"I would have done so, had all else failed."

"Jalil's right, dude, why wait for all else to fail? You could have had your boys take her out."

Galahad looked as if he must have misunderstood them. "But, surely you don't imagine that one of Arthur's knights, a Knight of the Round Table, son of Lancelot, would take the life of a woman? I live by the code, sir. By the code."

"Yeah. And now old Percy's dead, and Kay, and a bunch of other guys, too," Christopher said. "Didn't have to happen."

Galahad laughed, almost regretfully. "I am a creature of myth and legend, sir. I am what I must be, real or unreal, man or . . . or mere imagining.

I am a knight. Brave and true. Enemy to dragons, defender of maidens, servant of honor. I am what I must be. No more, no less."

We were chatting. Like people standing on the train tracks who can hear the train coming but are acting cool. Or maybe just psychotic. Death was coming, and we were discussing what we might have done.

I was watching Galahad's youthful face, a face that might have lived a thousand years, and saw his eyes focus past me on the rising mass of the god who had come to kill us all.

"Loki," Galahad said.

I turned, dread slowing my every movement. He appeared a little at a time as he climbed the hill. He was smiling. Happy. Doing what he enjoyed doing, I suppose. He sensed victory. He would get his witch, and then he would escape Ka Anor and Everworld and enter the real world.

He was fighting for his life. He was not going to be scared away.

Larger and larger he loomed. He raised one boot up and over the crumbled wall and slammed it down with such force that we jerked and jumped like bugs on a drumskin.

"Well, hello, Galahad, and you, Gawain. I'd heard you were mortally wounded, Galahad. An exaggeration, I see." He peered close. "But not much of an exaggeration. Now. Give me the witch and you can go riding off on one of your ludicrous quests. Surely there is some maiden in distress somewhere."

"I must decline, Great Loki," Galahad said with a deferential nod.

"Then I will kill you."

"That may be."

Loki reached down, wrapped his hand around the base of a sapling nearly his own height, and ripped it up. Dirt clung to the roots. He shook it, knocking some of the dirt loose, then threw it sideways at us.

Galahad swept his sword upward and sliced the sapling in two. It passed us by harmlessly. But that was Galahad's last blow. The sudden exertion ripped half a dozen stitches from the wound in his stomach.

He collapsed, clutching his sword hilt with one hand, his stomach with the other.

I knelt beside him. Tried to hold the wound shut.

Loki took three bounding, eager steps. He had grown no larger, at least; he stood twice the height of a tall man. But he was filled with palpable energy, untouched, unscarred, all wounds healed and forgotten.

Gawain yelled and rushed him.

David reached over and grabbed Galahad's sword. "With your permission, sir?" he asked gently.

"So long as you strike the foe," Galahad gritted.

Gawain whirled and brought his blade sideways, slashing, a blow that should have bitten clear through Loki's leg. Instead it hit, cut, drew freezing black blood, and stuck. Gawain tugged but couldn't pull it free.

David held Galahad's sword high, stabbing-style, running full out and yelling. Loki swept him aside with a brutal slap that threw David twenty feet into the tent.

"To me!" Loki yelled, and there came an answering roar of troll voices. So many. Too many. And now they appeared, head and shoulders first, massed and rushing over the wall, an avalanche of animated stone, hideous living statues.

The handful of men fell back almost without a fight. It was hopeless. Some ran. More ran. They fled past us, brushing by me in their panic.

The tidal wave of brutish, stone-handed creatures came on at a lumbering run. Seconds. That's all I had left. Seconds of life.

Life flashing before my eyes? Yes, no. Disjointed images, here and there, a fractured dream, all drenched with the sickness of dread. I was going to die.

"My lady," Galahad said. He was holding something for me. A knife. A dagger. Hilt toward me. Did he think I would stop the trolls? Did he think I would stop Loki?

No. Oh, God. It was for me. For me to use on myself.

CHAPTER
XXII

I took the knife. But my arm could not support the weight. I didn't have the strength, no strength at all. My arm hung limp, dagger hanging by my fingertips.

All over. What would happen? What was death like?

Then a loud voice began to chant. A rhythmic sound.

> "Ancient Stones,
> Broken Bones,
> Mend and grow,
> Ancient Stones.
> Wizard's tower,
> Upward flower,
> Ancient Stones,
> Hear again your master's voice."

A second wave of trolls was coming over the wall. They never made it. The wall had begun to grow. Trolls half over suddenly howled in pain as the wall grew beneath them.

All around, all around the oval of stone, the walls were growing, pushing up through the accumulation of grass and mold and lichen and moss. Fresh, white stone, stark in the darkness, then yellowed by reflected firelight.

The tower whose ruins we'd camped within was growing again.

Merlin stood there, shining from an inner light, hands held high, eyes wide and seeing something no one else saw. He was uplifted, chanting, repeating the incantation.

The rocks grew. Piled up as if some invisible giant were stacking them up at impossible speed.

The walls surrounded us, thirty feet high, but too late. Dozens of trolls were trapped inside with us. And Loki. Galahad down, Gawain disarmed, the men-at-arms panicked and outnumbered by the trolls. Too late, Merlin, too late.

"I warned you, Loki, that you were far from home," Merlin said. "I built this tower seven hundred years ago. It has since given way to the decay of time, but yet will it answer my commands."

He sounded confident but I could see that Merlin, too, had used up his last ounce of strength.

He fell to his knees, his arms dropped, his voice failed.

"Very good, Merlin, very impressive," Loki acknowledged. "But not enough."

I didn't know what to do. Merlin looked at me, right at me, his eyes sad and weary and defeated. His lips formed a single, soundless word.

"Door."

I looked around. There was no door in the tower walls. The only way out was straight up.

I looked helplessly at the wizard and shook my head. He looked annoyed, despite everything. He turned his head only slightly, toward the tent.

No, behind the tent. He'd left an escape route. Of course. Loki was twice the size of a man. The door would allow us through, but block him, for a while at least.

"Christopher. Jalil. Get ready."

"What?" Christopher demanded.

"When I say run, follow me. Sir Galahad, you're coming, too."

"We can't run, he'll just catch us," Christopher said harshly. "We gotta just see if he can understand, you know?"

"Fine, you stay and give up," I snapped. "We are leaving."

Loki reached down and yanked Gawain's sword out of his leg. He grabbed it like a knife and went for Merlin. Everything was happening at once. The trolls falling on the remaining men-at-arms. Slaughter. Merlin backing away. Loki's laugh. A scared, sobbing voice, mine.

Merlin had failed. We were not saved, and now Merlin himself was desperately fending off Loki's taunting thrusts, a cat to Loki's mouse.

The wind kicked up suddenly, grabbing at my hair, my clothes. Some strange natural feature of the open tower had created a wind, or maybe Loki had. It swirled within the enclosure like a tornado. Faster, warmer . . .

"There!" David yelled, face uplifted, arm pointing straight.

I looked up.

Dragon!

The dragon swooped closer, round and round at the top of the tower, closer and closer, the wind of its wings warmer and warmer.

Loki hesitated, unsure of how to respond to this new fact. And then, the dragon breathed.

Liquid fire sprayed from the dragon's mouth. Flew through the air. A red and orange stream, powerful as the spray of a firehose. It blistered the air. It splashed against Loki's upturned face, drenched the god in napalm, turning him into a walking, living, screaming torch, a pillar of fire that staggered blindly around inside the tower.

"Now," Merlin cried. "Run. Save Galahad. Gawain, go."

"I think not, good wizard," Gawain said. "I'll stay a while."

I grabbed Jalil's hand, guided it to Galahad. Pleaded, "Help me."

We grabbed the knight under his arms. Christopher grabbed one of his feet. We began running, as fast as we could while dragging a man.

The tent burst into flames.

Running, and David joined us, and running, while Galahad protested feebly, and my ears were filled by Loki's screams and the dragon's explosive fire and tornado wind.

A door. I burst through first, walking backward. Galahad scraping behind. Into the clear, out of the heat, and down winding steps, down to where the dark woods pressed close. Woods that might yet be filled with trolls.

David dropped Galahad's leg and stepped out in front, sword held ready.

Troll.

David raised his sword, Galahad's sword. "You know, I've had it with you things," he said. He ran straight for the troll.

The troll fell back, unwilling to fight. Why?

I heard Loki's high-pitched cries. Screams at a supernatural volume. Screams of pain and rage but no fear.

Of course. The troll heard it, too. The troll saw the wild flames whooshing up above the tower walls. His lord and master was in some kind of deep trouble.

We kept going, running, staggering more like it.

"Stop. Stop. I have to rest," I said.

We dropped Galahad, not gently.

"Now what?" Christopher asked. "Is Loki done for?"

"No," Galahad gasped. "Loki can be hurt, weakened, but not killed by mortal man or beast."

"He was looking pretty well-done back at the barbecue," Christopher said.

"Lose yourselves in the forest. Escape."

"We're saving your life, Galahad," David said. "Just play along."

"No. Find the witch. Keep her from Loki. Keep her from Ka Anor. You have done all you can do, and more."

I tried to see the wound in his belly, but it was too dark. I felt for it. Galahad took my hand and pushed it away.

"I have been wounded many times, my lady. I will survive."

"We're not leaving you here in the middle of nowhere. Period."

"You cannot travel with me. This day is a terrible defeat. Merlin, if he lives, will be weakened for weeks or months. You must —"

His words trailed off, lost in the gathering wind that dropped down on us from the sky.

The dragon stooped like a bird of prey, talons out and down, ready to seize Galahad.

"Hey, leave him alone!" I yelled up at the monster. "He's hurt."

The dragon landed lightly, almost delicately beside the trail. The fire dribbled from its mouth, illuminating my friends and Galahad in orange-black, Halloween colors.

"Hurt, is he?" the dragon wondered in its basso profundo voice. "Hurt but not yet dead."

"No, not dead," I said.

The dragon rumbled, thoughtful, amused. His snake's face twisted in a grimace that might have been a smile. Yellow cat's eyes were greedy, triumphant. "Galahad, at my mercy at last. Too badly wounded to raise an arm against me."

"Let him go," I pleaded. "You're on the same side. Merlin and Galahad are friends."

"The enemy of my enemy is my friend," Jalil

said. "The same should be true of friends. The friend of my friend is my friend."

The dragon laughed, greatly amused. "Friend? Merlin is no friend of mine. What nonsense have you told these Old World fools, Galahad?"

"Give me my sword," Galahad whispered tersely to David. Then, in as loud a voice as he could manage, a hoarse shout, "The dragon fights for gold, like all his kind."

"Yes, for gold. Why else? For honor? For chivalry? I will be paid for this night's work. A king's ransom in treasure, gold and silver and diamonds and rubies. I will be well paid for giving that upstart god Loki a lesson in humility, but Loki is no enemy of mine."

The dragon half walked, half writhed to Galahad. The fire dripped from his lips within inches of Galahad's upturned face.

"Farewell, Galahad, dragon-killer."

"My sword!" Galahad cried, desperate. "My sword! Let me die with my sword in my hand."

David darted in and placed the sword in Galahad's weak hand. Galahad struggled to his feet. I rushed to help him.

"You can't do this, he's weak, he's injured," I said. "He can't even fight back, it's cowardly. If you want to fight him, wait till —"

Galahad put his hand over my mouth. "Hush, my lady. My story is at an end. At long last, my story is over. Yours is not."

He pushed me back, hard, groaning with the pain of the effort, he shoved me back. I fell, sprawled.

The dragon breathed.

CHAPTER
XXIII

We tried to give him a decent burial. There wasn't much time with us fearing the trolls and Loki. But we couldn't leave him there by the side of the trail.

He was easy to move. He weighed very little after the flames burned themselves out.

We tried digging but had no tools except for Galahad's sword. So we found whatever rocks we could and piled them till he was mostly covered. He'd lived centuries. And now he was dead by the side of a path. A pile of rocks.

"We should bury the man with his sword," Christopher said.

"Yeah. We should," David agreed. "But it's the only weapon we have."

"He needs a cross," I said.

"We've taken up all the time we can," David said.

"He's getting a cross," I said.

Jalil used Excalibur to cut notches in some sticks. So Galahad got a cross.

When that was done the others all looked expectantly at me.

We were all tired. All jumpy. All sick with memories.

"I don't know the words," I said. "I don't know what to say."

"Sing him a song, then," Christopher said.

"I don't know any," I said. "I mean, what do you sing at a funeral? The masses I know, all choral, I mean." I made a sound of frustration. David was anxious to get going, and he was right.

Then it occurred to me. Not a perfect song. Not something in Latin, the way it ought to be. But maybe it would do. It was a song from *Rent*.

"Okay," I said, just as David and Jalil were turning away. I took a couple of deep breaths. My voice was ragged. I sounded pretty bad, definitely not up for a solo. But it was something. And he deserved something.

So I sang "Without You."

"That's it," I said. I was crying. "Not exactly right, is it? We barely knew him. And we won't die because he's dead. We barely knew him. So why . . . is it just that he was nice and good-looking and brave? Why does it hurt me, him being gone?"

"He was a legend," David said. "We didn't know him, but we knew what he represented. He was good standing up against evil. He was the strong man defending the weak. He was brave when the odds were against him. What else is a man supposed to be? What else is he supposed to do?"

" 'We shall not see his like again.' Shakespeare, I think," Jalil said.

"Yes," I said. "I don't remember which play."

David knelt down beside the grave. He held the sword out over the stones. "I'll try to be worthy of your sword."

I shook my head wonderingly. Every time I thought I understood David he surprised me. But I guess that's true of people generally. You never know them, not all the way.

"Let's get moving," David said.

And somehow, despite everything, despite all that had happened with Senna, we followed him.

We walked through the night. I was too tired to feel tired. My legs moved. That's all I knew, my legs were still moving.

We found a tiny creek and drank all we could

hold, then we followed the creek. No idea where we were going, of course, no idea except to put Loki and his trolls and Merlin and Galahad all behind us.

We walked till I tripped on a root and just couldn't get up again. I didn't want to be the weak one, the official girl. But I was done walking.

"Let's stop here," David said, making the best of it.

Jalil and Christopher collapsed on the ground beside me. It was cold and damp and I was wearing a dress and little else. I lay back, staring up at the trees, realizing that I could see the outlines of the branches, which meant dawn was coming.

I lay there and felt the wetness seep through the thin fabric, and I just didn't care. I wanted sleep. I wanted sleep. I slung my backpack under my head to make a thin pillow.

"Anyone wakes me up, I'll . . . I'll something," I warned.

"See you on the other side," Christopher said.

But sleep wouldn't come. Not right away. I was cold, and then I started shivering. A light rain began to fall, barely more than dew.

I sat up on my backpack and wept with my face in my hands. Why was this happening? Why was my life this way? Why couldn't it just have gone on being the way it was?

The rain stopped. The sun came up above the trees. I resigned myself to never sleeping again. And then I was home.

Chapter
XXIV

It was Sunday afternoon. The same Sunday
that had seen me yelling in church. There was no
making sense of the synchronization of time between the real world and Everworld. It seemed to
slip forward, back, faster, slower.

I crossed over and found I was at the bookstore
downtown, the Barnes and Noble. I was upstairs
at a table near the mythology section.

I had a book open in front of me, others piled
up. I was reading about Galahad. Had been reading about him for the last hour.

The real-world me received the updated news
from the Everworld me. Galahad dead. Merlin,
no one knew. Loki? Still presumably looking for
Senna, who had managed to slip out of camp
while everyone was busy fighting to keep her
from Loki.

I was embarrassed by the emotion I'd felt over the death of Galahad. Glad to still be alive. Even glad that Senna was still alive.

My memories merged, becoming the mind of a single person again. Memories of reading the story of Galahad, and memories of seeing its final chapter.

What was I doing reading about him? Everworld shouldn't matter to me, the real me. Let that other April deal with that. I wasn't going to let it seep into my life, eat away at my life.

And yet, I'd been reading about Galahad.

"I told them we'd find you here," Jalil said. He and David and Christopher all sat down. David grabbed a chair from another table.

They looked strange. They were dressed like normal people. So was I, for that matter. We were warm and clothed and dry and there was no cut under Jalil's eye. Clean hair and faces, brushed teeth. They looked strange.

"We all here?" Christopher asked.

"I've been here. This is me," I said a little tersely. Then I softened. "But yeah, I have had an update."

Jalil tapped the book. "What did that tell you?"

I shrugged. "I know why he and Gawain had the same memories of the Holy Grail. The story originally had Gawain as the quester. But Gawain was seen as a more pagan figure, so it was rewritten with Galahad as the star."

"And there never was a real Galahad?" Christopher asked.

"I don't know. No one does. Maybe they were all real, or partly real. Or maybe real doesn't mean what we think it does, I so totally don't know. I don't know much of anything anymore."

I closed the book.

"So now what?" Christopher asked.

No one answered.

"Now what?" he pressed. "Come on, we need to think about what we're doing. We can't just keep walking around over there. We can't just keep stumbling into one mess after another. Sooner or later our luck runs out. We need a plan."

"You have a suggestion?" Jalil asked.

"I suggest we find Senna and make her send us back here. Permanently. Simple. David, you can stay over there. I know you love all that. Me, personally, I'm for getting out. Hey, it's been fun hanging with the Vikings and almost getting my heart cut out by the Aztecs and playing hide-and-seek with Loki, but vacation is over."

"We don't know where she is," Jalil pointed out. "Senna. We don't know where she is."

"Okay, so we find her," Christopher said.

"That's my point. We need a plan, a goal. She's the goal. She's the only way this all stops. We get her, keep her from Loki, and bye-bye, Everworld. It's the only way, man."

"What about the people there? The people in Everworld?"

They all looked at me in surprise. I'd surprised myself.

"Say what?" Jalil snapped.

"Look, it's stupid, I guess. I mean, I guess it's stupid. But here's the thing: Galahad was a good person. So is Gawain. And maybe Merlin, too. I mean, Everworld isn't all just psycho gods and cannibals and trolls and —"

I fell silent as a girl I knew slightly walked past.

"I mean, those are real people. At least over there they are. And some of them are good people."

"So what?" Jalil asked.

"So maybe that changes things," I said.

"Changes nothing," Christopher said in a warning tone. "Listen: It changes nothing."

"Okay," I said. "What do we do after we force Senna to let us out?"

"We get some beer and party, and we get on with our lives," Christopher said.

"And Senna's still there? Still in Everworld? Still a gateway for Loki or Huitzilopoctli?"

"Oh, no. No, no." Christopher was shaking his finger at me, back and forth. "No, no, no."

David, on the other hand, was grinning. "You're right. We get through the gate and then leave it open? That means we don't escape Everworld, Everworld follows us here. We have Huitzilopoctli stomping around Old Orchard Mall ripping hearts out. Dragons on the loose. Loki."

I nodded, hating what I was thinking. But unable to avoid thinking it. "There are some good people over there. Maybe Merlin's right. The good people can get together, get the bad guys to at least go along, stop Ka Anor, which means the creeps like Loki aren't looking to escape."

Jalil was giving me serious fish-eye. "So all we'd have to do is solve all the problems of Everworld, take out Ka Anor — who is so bad he scares Loki half to death — and then we can come home, pat ourselves on the back, and no problem?"

David nodded. "Yeah. That's exactly right."

Christopher leaned forward across the table, his voice low and intense. "We have one sword, a backpack with a few pathetic pieces of junk, we're lost, we know nothing, not even how long a day is, or what the land is like, or . . . are you crazy? Are you nuts?"

"Christopher, we're there anyway, okay? I don't like it, I wish it hadn't happened, but we're there. Senna is our way home, but our way home is everyone else's gateway to the destruction of our world. There is no escape. Not really. So we have to change the world. We have to change Everworld."

Christopher said something rude. David laughed happily and slapped the table. Jalil looked down at the book, then at me.

"That blood transfusion. Guess it went both ways, huh?"

We split up after that. No one wanted to talk. No one was happy with me, except for David, and his happiness just depressed me.

We went our separate ways. Me to my home to hook up with my parents. We did a barbecue in the backyard and had some neighbors over. I ate grilled vegetables.

I talked on the phone to Mario. We made a date for the next weekend.

I did some homework. Then I rehearsed some of the numbers from *Rent* in front of my mirror. And when I tried to sing "Without You" I cried.

I stayed up late watching TV. And when I went to bed at last I knew that I would wake up right there, warm and rested in my room. And that I would also wake up wet and miserable and scared in a place that could not possibly exist.

But did.

EVER WORLD

#IV

REALM OF THE REAPER

David raised his sword to his shoulder, Sammy Sosa waiting for a fast one down the middle.

The pig ran. David swung. The pig hit him hard, David spun and fell clutching his leg and cried out in pain. I saw a splash of bright red.

Christopher yelled a curse and then the pig was on me. I stabbed downward at it, missed, stuck my sword point in the ground, no time to yank it back out, the pig knocked me down like a bowling ball hitting the last standing pin. . . . The pig was on me. I shoved. Hands against squirming muscle, not fat. . . .

The tusks, the curved, nasty teeth, that snout, inches from my face. . . . The pig was going to kill me.